MURDER WAS FLEXING ITS MUSCLES

Madame Natasha's body building salon promised to get Hardy into top shape—but from the moment he stripped for action, he could see that things were shaping up far differently than he had expected.

Natasha and her band of beautiful helpers had their own ideas how to build up a man—but when exercise turned into sexercise, Hardy had no trouble getting right into the swing of things. Then a lovely lady teacher was taught a lethal lesson by a master of murder, and the sensuous sleuth knew that once again he would have to mix business with pleasure.

Playtime was over—and slaytime had begun. . . .

HUNG UP TO DIE

by Martin Meyers

AN AUTHORS GUILD BACKINPRINT.COM EDITION

Hung Up To Die

All Rights Reserved © 1976, 2000 by Martin Meyers

No part of this book may be reproduced or transmitted in any form
or by any means, graphic, electronic, or mechanical, including photocopying,
recording, taping, or by any information storage or retrieval system,
without the permission in writing from the publisher.

AN AUTHORS GUILD BACKINPRINT.COM EDITION

Published by iUniverse.com, Inc.

For information address:
iUniverse.com, Inc.
620 North 48th Street, Suite 201
Lincoln, NE 68504-3467
www.iuniverse.com

Originally published by Popular Library

ISBN: 0-595-09007-9

Printed in the United States of America

CHAPTER ONE

⚜ Patrick Hardy waited for the cross traffic to pass, and accelerated the VW. He got up to fourth gear as quickly as possible and kept a nice, steady pace of sixty-five to seventy miles an hour. It had been a great vacation.

Hardy was on his way back to New York City. He had stopped for lunch and was now looking for an entrance back onto the throughway. While the upper portion of his brain concentrated on the problem at hand, a tiny mental closet in a lower corner housed and cherished the memory of the summer that had just passed.

His intention of staying in town during the summer had been changed by the heat and air pollution, and Con Edison constantly badgering him in the media to use his air-conditioner as seldom as possible to conserve watts. This combined annoyance drove him out of the city and up to Maine.

The Lodge, as it was called, offered accommodations in the new hotel or in private cabins. Hardy had, consistent with his nature, chosen one of the cabins.

The memory of hot days and cold nights, and the lake at his back door, and the blazing fire for those nights was a pleasant one to dwell on.

That upper section of his mind warned him that he was going too fast, and he dropped down to fifty while the part of his brain that was doing the dwelling hopped around and found other memories: the solitude of the cabin, the convenience of the bar in the hotel restaurant, the restaurant, with its Maine-style smorgasbord, New England boiled beef and Indian pudding.

The truck that brought fresh kindling every morning for his fireplace.

The cleaning women with their Yankee accents and straightforward attitudes.

The steaks and baked potatoes cooked in the cabin.

Louise.

Louise had been staying in the cabin up and across the road. She knocked on his door because she couldn't get her fire started and, after that one time, never left—at least, not as long as their vacations lasted.

HARDY

They swam at night in the lake and then made love in the cold water. Even now, with only part of his memory working on it, Hardy was amazed that he had been able to function, considering what cold water had done at other times to that important part of his anatomy.

But they had made love and then, freezing and shivering, run back into his cabin for scotch and steaks. Afterward, their stomachs sated but other appetites still demanding, they'd made love again, and in the morning, strolled down hand-in-hand to the hotel dining room for a breakfast of country ham and eggs.

The days were spent sailing, and loafing, and eating and making love. The nights were spent making love.

It had been a great vacation.

As he mentally retraced the experience, his eye caught sight of a girl hitchhiking, and his memories and fantasies fused.

Hardy jammed on the brakes and pressed the stick down and into reverse.

The girl got in and announced that her name was Lucy, and that she just wanted a lift for a couple of miles down to where her trailer was.

L for Louise, L for Lucy. Hardy thought of it as a good omen as he examined the pretty face under the sandy hair and the ripe young breasts under only a tee shirt.

"There's where I want," said Lucy. "Thanks."

Instead of dropping her at the roadside, Hardy turned in to where the trailer was moored.

"Where's your car?" he asked.

"At the local garage, being fixed for the ten-millionth time." The girl got out and smiled. "Thanks again—unless you want to come in for a minute, and have a cup of coffee, or a drink." She looked at him quizzically. "Or a reefer."

He laughed. "You wouldn't be putting me on? You're not a narc, are you?"

"Hey," she answered, "I'm the one who should be asking you that. You're cool. Come on in. They're rolled and waiting."

As the two of them turned on in the close confines of the trailer, she said, "You sure could have fooled me." She studied the well-built six-foot private detective. "If there was one man in this world I would not have spotted as a head, it would have been you."

They giggled at her remark and soared higher and higher. So high, that Hardy barely heard the car coming to a stop outside the trailer. But he was having too much fun to care.

"Hey," she said, "it's too hot in here. Take off your shirt—I'm going to take off mine."

The tentative erection that had been forming ever since they entered the trailer was no longer tentative. Paying attention to nothing but those lovely young breasts with their jaunty, up-turned nipples, Hardy all but tore the buttons from his shirt—and the young man entering the trailer behind him all but tore the head off his shoulders.

The clout on the back of the neck stunned and awakened Hardy at the same time. His high was gone and his reflexes were in working order. With no time to be afraid, he turned and dove at his assailant's knees. The young giant fell and got right up, and all six-and-a-half feet of him came after Hardy. The younger man jabbed with a left that Hardy avoided. When the right hand came out, Hardy ducked, but at the last minute reversed, and thrust his head back up and clipped the kid right on the chin.

The monster bellowed and shook off the blow, and put two meathooks out and grabbed at Hardy. Hardy side-stepped but not fast enough, and the meathooks connected with his carcass.

Out through the open door and onto the ground. Luckily, it was grassy. Grassy—there was a joke there someplace.

The giant came rushing out after him. He picked Hardy up and held him with his left hand, setting him up for a hammering from his right. Hardy bit the holding hand and avoided the other. In the second's respite this gave him, he clasped both of his own hands together and used them to chop at the youngster's neck. Effective, but not enough. Hardy kicked him in the groin and then in the chin.

Giant, in one last effort, reared back and ran

right over Hardy. Hardy jumped to his feet and turned, waiting for the new attack. There was none. The young man had not turned to finish the fight; instead, he had kept on running, and was now in the car and starting it up. Hardy ran after him. By this time, the boy was on the road and burning rubber.

Hardy looked after him, fire in his eye. Then the fire was gone and retroactive fear took over. He stood up quickly and urinated on a bush. Then he spit and swallowed several times, to keep from throwing up.

He walked back to the trailer, slightly favoring his left leg. The girl was still there, and so were those delightful breasts.

Hardy switched gears immediately. The giant was forgotten, and so was the slight ache in his knee, but the high was back, and so was his erection. He sat down and enjoyed himself, just looking.

She walked over to him, placing one of those firm young breasts into his waiting mouth.

He unzipped her pants and heard her say, "Where were we, before we were so rudely interrupted?"

As he got dressed, he wasn't sure whether he had been the near-victim of a roughhouse badger-game or just an innocent bystander caught between two lovers, but he wanted to get out of there before Gargantua returned.

He turned to say good-bye, but Lucy was

someplace else in her head and would never even notice his absence.

After turning on his key and shifting into first, he hit his brakes and turned the engine off. On a hunch, he hopped out and checked his luggage compartment. It was unlocked, and his bags were gone.

It had been a badger-game—and more.

One of two things had happened: the guy had taken his things before pouncing on him, or the girl had taken them while he was chasing her friend. Hardy went back to the trailer. Lucy was still in never-never land. It was a small trailer, and he found his bags quickly.

As he passed her, he stopped, put down the bags, kissed each nipple and said, "Thanks for the merry-go-round ride. Tell your friend, better luck next time."

CHAPTER TWO

⚜ Driving the rest of the way back to New York, the only thing that annoyed Hardy was the twinge in his left leg. The damaged knee wasn't in as good shape as he had thought. He worried about it, and wondered if what he felt wasn't a sign that perhaps he ought to go and see the therapist Dr. Nesor had recommended.

Hardy concentrated on trying to remember her name. "Natasha Tamarova," he said out loud. Somewhere on his desk or in one of the drawers, was a slip of paper the surgeon had given him, with her address on it. He would look for it when he got to his apartment.

When the radio drifted and he started picking up a station in New York in addition to the Boston station, he knew he'd be home soon. He adjusted the dial and, as was to be expected, the announcer told him about traffic tie-ups on the Cross-Bronx Expressway.

Despite the radio, the road was clear when he got there, and it was smooth riding all the way.

He parked his bug in the bus stop in front of his private entrance and went around to the main building to pick up his accumulated mail. Pete, the doorman, gave it to him, all neatly held together with rubber bands.

"How was the vacation, Mr. Hardy?"

"Eventful, Pete, eventful," and he went back around the corner to his apartment. As he started for the door, his eye caught something. The car that had been parked in the position behind him was gone, and so was one of the VW's tail lights. Hardy examined the damage and cursed, but it had happened before. He dismissed the incident and opened the outside door to his place. He walked down the hallway and thought about buying a new VW and having a Porsche engine installed, just as he had read that Paul Newman had done years before.

His wishful thinking was ended by the complexities involved in undoing all the locks and alarms on the inside door.

He dropped his luggage in the inside hall and his mail on the desk in his office, reminding himself to look for that piece of paper Dr. Nesor had given him, with Natasha what's-her-name's address.

A visit to the john and one to the kitchen.

Laura, his housekeeper, had come through. The kitchen was stocked with all his favorite goodies. Loaded with a ham and cheese on rye, a large bag of potato chips and a bottle of ginger ale, he parked himself on the brown-and-black chaise in his office and flicked on the tv.

After eating and watching the tail end of *Captain's Paradise*, he burped and dialed Denise Shaw's number.

Like most of the women Hardy knew, Denise was in show business. He had met her while working on a case. The summer stock tour she had signed for turned out to be short-lived, so she had kept Sherlock Holmes, his black standard poodle, for him while he had gone off to Maine—and Louise.

"Hi, Denny," he said when she answered the phone.

"Pat. You're back. Oh, I'm so glad you're home. I know you wanted to be alone, but I wish you had let me come along with you. Did you get a good rest?"

"Yeah, sure, fine."

"You lying bastard. You probably screwed everything that moved."

"Shut up and come on over, and bring my friend with you."

"Okay. I don't know who missed you more, me or him. Bye. Wait a minute! Am I just a dog-sitter and delivery-girl, or am I invited for dinner?"

"Dinner and more, if you'll stay."

"I'll stay, all right—big boy," she added mockingly, and hung up the phone.

Hardy rubbed his hands together and set about preparing one of his favorite meals: chicken à la Kiev, spiced peaches and wild rice.

When the girl and the dog arrived, they both made a fuss over him and kissed him and touched him, but it was Denise who said, "I think you put on a little weight during the summer."

"No, just the way these pants fit," he answered, not wanting to admit that he had gone from 185 to 200 pounds. The double thought in his head concerned a resolve to go on a diet—after tonight's dinner—and starting working out again on a regular basis.

"Don't kid me," she said, and grabbed at the slight roll at his waist. He avoided her reach.

"I'm in great a shape as ever. Come into the bedroom, and I'll prove it to you."

"Later," the cute little girl promised. "But I bet you can't do ten chin-ups without breathing heavy."

"Come on." And they went to the little gym adjacent to his bedroom. He did fifteen chin-ups and worked very hard not to show her what a chore it was.

As they started back to the living room

through the bedroom, he fell on the bed and changed his mind about admitting his fatigue, or at least he pretended to. "You're right, that knocked me out. Why don't you come over here and keep me company?"

"You horny son of a bitch," she smiled. "Don't I even get a drink first?"

"The red wine's in the pantry—and bring me back a Kahlua on the rocks, and cheat it with a little water."

She pouted at him and curtsied, and went to get the drinks. While she was gone, he took the phone off the hook and put it into the night table drawer. Then he switched on the radio to an FM music station while he stripped himself and the neatly made-up bed. He was under the covers when she returned.

Denise took in the situation and kept her distance while she sipped her drink.

"Either you're very anxious, or you're hiding under there so I won't see how fat you are."

Her remark was an immediate turn-off. He lost his erection and his knee began to ache. With a frown on his face, he beckoned for his drink, which she gave him. "Get off that fat stuff, Den. You don't hear me constantly commenting on how flat your chest is."

"Say it all you want," she said, completely unperturbed. "Who needs more than a handful?"

"You haven't even got that."

Denise still wasn't bothered. "I'm not

impressed." She paused and said, "Come on, Pat, quit it. I'm sorry if I hurt your feelings." She sat on the bed next to him. "Forgive me?"

She put her drink down to kiss him and, within minutes, she was out of her clothes and in bed with him.

"Slowly, slowly," she said.

"I know."

And they kissed and petted and fondled for a long time. Hardy had been ready the minute she had joined him under the sheets, and now so was she.

They rocked and writhed and interwove, finding each other's places and applying the proper gratification, climbing up and up until her nails started working on his back, and they climaxed together, and fell into a pleasant, idyllic sleep.

He was awakened by the sound of running water. He drank the hot tea she offered and followed her to the bathroom and the tub.

"How's your leg?" Denise asked.

"Pretty good," Hardy answered, as he eased himself into the hot water. "Ah, that feels great."

"Okay?"

"Okay. Come on in, Den, the water's fine. The leg's not as good as it should be, though. I think I'll have to go to a therapist for a while."

She was in the tub, scrubbing his back.

"You've got a couple of nasty bruises. What did you run into, a truck?"

"You did it, in the grip of passion," he evaded, not wanting to explain or lie about Lucy and her giant boy friend.

"What the hell are you doing?" he asked as she rubbed shampoo into his scalp.

"Washing your hair. It's filthy."

"It's easier," he told her, "if you do it while you shower."

"But my way's more fun. Here, you do me."

He enjoyed the lemon smell and the game of being two kids playing in the tub as they frolicked and scrubbed and got soap all over everything.

Later, while he cut into the chicken à la Kiev and watched with satisfaction as the chive-green-flecked golden butter squirted out as it was supposed to, "Pat?"

"What?"

"There's a jazz concert. Will you take me?"

"Sure. When do you want to go?"

"Anytime this week," she answered.

"Fine," he said, adding wild rice and peaches to his happy stomach. "I have to go downtown tomorrow to see about starting my therapy. I'll pick up the tickets then. Remind me in the morning—you are staying?"

She filled his wineglass. "Try and get rid of me."

They watched part of an old Rock Hudson

desert epic, and then switched channels to watch Bette Midler doing an Andrews Sisters routine.

"Look at her," said Denise.

"I know," said Hardy, as the performer segued into a sad new song that was even better than the first number. "She's great."

"I don't mean that. I mean, you're right, but she's proof that I can make it."

"I don't want to put you down, Den, but she's got that little extra something. Of course, I've never seen you work."

"Oh," she pouted. "You civilians. You don't understand. Just a few years ago, she and I were working as extras on the same film."

"So?"

"So, she's proof that I can make it. She did it, why can't I?"

"I don't know? Why can't you?"

The little redhead rolled over and pretended to go to sleep. A boring author came out on the talk show, and Hardy switched back to Rock Hudson and his derring-do. When the movie was over, he turned off the set and the light.

In a few moments Denise snuggled closer and said, "Pat, I am going to make it, aren't I?"

"Sure, baby, sure you are," and he held her in his arms until she fell asleep.

CHAPTER THREE

⊗ In the morning, Denise seemed to have forgotten her mood of the night before, and didn't complain when Hardy chased her out of the kitchen to make them a real breakfast.

While she sipped coffee and he demolished a large plate of wheatcakes, he checked over his mail. One of the items was the summer edition of his college alumni bulletin. He would read it on the bus downtown.

He checked his service. Nothing of any importance.

They dressed and were ready to leave. He had found Dr. Nesor's memo on Natasha Tamarova.

The phone rang. Hardy put on his business voice and answered, "Trouble Limited, Patrick Hardy speaking."

"Hi Pat," said Steve Macker, an old friend

and a sometime actor and sometime leg-man for Trouble Limited.

"Hi, yourself," said Hardy. "What's been happening to you?"

"Nothing much. The Coast is dead. I was thinking of coming back to New York. How's the action there?"

"Do you mean show business, detective business or women?"

"All three."

"I'll give you a quick answer. Two bads and one good."

"That's enough for me," said Macker. "I hope that good applies to women. I've been looking for an excuse to get out of tinsel town for quite a while." Hardy heard a noise. "I've got someone waiting," said Macker. "I'll see you when I see you." He hung up.

Hardy returned the phone to its cradle, and while they went across the street to catch the bus, he explained who Macker was and warned Denise to keep away from him.

She smiled happily at his possessiveness. "If he's as good as he sounds, warn him to keep away from me. I might attack him if he comes too close."

They talked until Forty-Fifth Street, where Hardy got off to walk east. Denise was staying on to go to her apartment in the Village. "Don't forget the tickets," she shouted.

"I won't," he answered, and shoved the college bulletin in his back pocket as he began his walk.

He took out Dr. Nesor's note and read what it had to say. The doctor had given two sets of directions. Since the first concerned using the 104 bus, Hardy skipped that and read the second, and did as it said.

He went to the Pan-Am Building, walking through all the hustle and bustle of people. Ascertaining where the down escalators were, he took them to Grand Central Terminal. More people coming and going, hustling and bustling. Hardy made the proper turns, or so he thought, got lost, went back to the foot of the escalator, and this time really made the proper turns and wound up in front of an elevator.

There was a sign proclaiming that the Natasha Tamarova Studio was on the ninth floor. Hardy pushed the button and waited. The elevator was a long time coming. The private detective pulled the college magazine from his pocket and leafed through it. He yawned as he barely glanced at items about kids from classes that came well after his.

The letters to the editor bore no signatures that he recognized. The class notes section went to the other extreme from the earlier items: Class of '22, '24, '26. The elevator arrived. He punched nine and read on. The only name that he knew was George Lassiter. George had graduated the same year he had. He was now doing very well in the feed and grain business in Oregon.

He got off the elevator and thought back. Lassiter had been second-string quarterback while Hardy had been the school's fat boy. Still, they had been friends of a sort. He shrugged and stuffed the magazine into a trash can and, instructed by another sign, climbed the remaining flight of stairs.

He was going to like this. There were all sorts of girls and women running around in tight-fitting leotards. There were some out-and-out dogs, but Hardy knew he could garner the wheat from the chaff, and the caliber of men present didn't seem to be any sort of competition. And—all the therapists and instructors were women.

"Hello, may I help you?"

He looked at her, and then had to force his eyes away to read her name tag: Faith Cade.

"Yes . . . Faith."

He smiled, she smiled. Hardy continued, "I'd like to see Natasha Tamarova. Dr. Nesor suggested I see her."

"Wait right here," said Faith Cade, indicating a bench. "I'll try to get her for you." The blonde smiled again, and walked among the exercisers until she came to another blonde. The second blonde was older, and long and lean. Hardy kept his eyes on Faith as she talked to the other woman. The younger girl was quite beautiful, and Hardy was contemplating a great many things.

Much to his disappointment, Faith Cade stayed, and the long, lean woman came toward him. Only as she got very close did Hardy realize how old she really was. Her body was that of a thirty-year-old, but she had to be at least sixty.

"How do you do?" she said, thrusting forth her hand and speaking with a slight Russian accent. "I am Natasha. How is Dr. Nesor?"

"Very well. He sends his regards."

"What seems to be your problem?"

"Cartilage was removed from my left knee, and the doctor thought you might be able to help me."

"Not might, can—if you are up to a little hard work. Good. I will speak to him later on the phone, and get filled in. In the meantime, each session is an hour long. You must be on time. You may wear dance tights or shorts and a tee shirt. No shoes in the studio, only dance slippers. I expect beginners to work at least two sessions a week. When would you like to start?"

"This week would be fine."

"Good. Lane!" she called, and a stunning brunette glided over. Her nameplate said Lane Peterson, and her body, though a little fuller, was just as stacked as Faith Cade's. Decisions, decisions, decisions, thought Hardy.

"Lane, this is Mr. Hardy."

The girl nodded.

Natasha continued, "Check the schedule, and see if we can start him this week." She turned back to him. "I shall start you off the first day, and then the others will take care of you. Good-bye," she added, and wheeled about to get back to her various duties. Hardy willingly followed Lane Peterson to a small office, where he filled out forms and paid for his first twelve sessions in advance. He received a booklet about the studio, and agreed to begin on Friday, at four o'clock.

"The schedule is flexible," Lane said. "Some people come at the same time all the time, but if you want, you can tell us when you're coming again at the end of each session, and I can write you in on the chart." She was pointing to the wall. The chart served a double purpose. It showed when clients were due, and when the staff was out to lunch or whatever.

Her chin was just a little pointy, but Hardy still wondered if he could make her.

Lane flashed a smile on and off, and said, "Be here Friday at four, then, and don't forget your costume. Oh, one more thing. They're repairing the women's dressing room—a pipe upstairs burst—so, for a while, we've only got one. Take off your shoes, and I'll show you."

She led him past a closet and a rear staircase to a room that had a homemade sign secured by a thumbtack. The sign was clock shaped, and had a single hand that could point to one of three designations: "Male," "Female," "Free." The hand now pointed to "Free." Lane knocked, anyway, before opening the door. The room was empty, and the girl showed him where the lockers were.

"There are no keys," she said. "But don't worry, we have a good clientele, to quote Natasha. Besides, you can check your cash and watch in the office. There's one shower, in the john, but since the dressing room has become co-ed, hardly anybody uses it. I do, because I can't wait to get home to wash up. Besides, a body's a body."

Hardy didn't know if that was just an honest statement or a prelude line. He decided to let it pass.

As they left the room, a shy man with a creased, gentle face waited for them to go by.

"Go ahead, Mr. Butler. You can go in."

The man's eyes twinkled. "Thank you, Miss Peterson. I wouldn't want to frighten any of the ladies." He turned the dial to "Male" and entered the room, closing the door securely behind him.

Lane led Hardy back to his shoes, and then went on about her job.

The elevator was so long in coming that, by the time it did arrive, Mr. Butler was there to join Hardy on his ride down.

He nodded. "Excuse me—I don't mean to seem inquisitive, but are you joining us?"

"Yes I am. Patrick Hardy."

"Hello. I'm Jackson Butler. Bad back."

"Huh?" Hardy exclaimed.

"I'm here for my back. They do wonders."

"With me, it's my knee."

"They'll fix you up in no time," said Butler. "Don't worry. And they're very nice people."

The elevator was at ground level.

"I'm sure they are," said Hardy. "Good-bye."

"Good-bye, nice meeting you." And soon the little man was lost in the crowd.

Rather than go through the Pan-Am Building again, Hardy searched for the subway entrance he knew was somewhere in the terminal. Just as he found it, he remembered about the tickets for the jazz concert, and went up to the street level instead.

He was on Forty-Second Street.

He was hungry, so he headed for the drugstore on the corner. Much to his pleased surprise, he bumped into Faith Cade just as they were both going in.

"Hello again."

"Hello," she said warily, her eyes showing no recognition.

He was crushed. "Patrick Hardy. We just met upstairs."

"Oh. I'm sorry, Mr. Hardy. I meet so many people each day."

"That's all right. Forget it. There are two seats over there."

The young blonde didn't seem to be that anxious to join him, but there were no other places available. They sat down and ordered.

Hardy was about to attempt conversation when the girl took out a copy of a script and started reading it. She stopped long enough to say, "Excuse me, but I have an audition later on, and I haven't had much chance to look this over."

"You an actress?" he asked foolishly. Without waiting for her to answer, he said, "Go ahead. Read on and good luck. I hope you get the part."

She stopped, in earnest this time, and showed him one of those pretty smiles she had exhibited up in the studio. "Thank you. Most people wouldn't have understood."

Their lunch came. They both ate silently, she studying her script and he studying her. Hardy finished before she did, but dawdled over his coffee so he could leave with her. He tried to pick up her check, but she wouldn't allow it.

Outside, he delayed moving so he could walk in any direction she chose, but she said, "Well, good-bye, Mr. Hardy. See you soon."

Disappointed at opportunities lost, Hardy merely stood there and mused about her. He thought he was getting his second chance of the day when he saw Lane Peterson coming out to the street, but the brunette was met almost immediately by a young stud with hair almost to his shoulders and a damn-you strut to his gait. They walked away. Hardy took a moment to muse again, and then decided it was time for him to move on, too.

After picking up the tickets for that Friday night, he checked his service. There was a message from Denise saying she would be a little late because she had an audition. He hadn't recalled talking to her about coming over, but he didn't mind. It seemed to be a busy day for young actresses.

He took in a movie and then grabbed a cab home.

As they were riding, he noticed a woman cab driver alongside. "Are there many women hacks?" he asked the driver.

"Maybe two hundred."

"Out of how many drivers?"

"Jeez, I don't know," said the driver, "About ninety thousand, I guess."

Hardy thought his last estimate was a little high, but didn't comment, except to say, "I couldn't do it. Too nerve-racking."

"Why shouldn't you?" said the driver. "Everybody and his brother has a hack license in this town. Why should you be different?"

"But I thought there weren't enough drivers?"

The driver took advantage of a red light to fill out his trip sheet and light a cigar. "I said they had licenses, I didn't say they were working at it."

"Oh, I see," said Hardy, not seeing at all. "You mean, people just get them and don't use them?"

"That's right—except when they want to pick up a few quick bucks, moonlighting, that's what they do, but not steady. They're crying for men at the garage."

"Well," said Hardy, trying to end the conversation, "it's a tough job. I wouldn't want to do it. My nerves couldn't stand it."

Now that the driver was talking, he wouldn't stop. "You're telling me it's tough. That's why I switched to the day shift. It's bad enough during the day, but at night, look out. I still carry this." He reached down under his seat and pulled out a length of pipe, which he showed Hardy. "Those plastic partitions won't do any good. You need something like this."

Hardy nodded.

The driver kept talking. "You know what they ought to do? Ban all traffic except cabs, buses and trucks. Remember that snow storm a few years back? Just cabs and buses. Even with the snow and ice, it was heaven."

"Hold it! Hold it!" yelled Hardy, but he was

too late, and they were a block past his apartment. He paid and got out quickly, stopping to check if he had left anything in his haste. After slamming the door and watching the cab leave, he decided that as long as he wasn't at his door, he would walk over to Broadway and get the paper. He bought the *Post* and the new *Playboy*, and methodically tore out all the extraneous pieces of cardboard that were sprinkled throughout the magazine to advertise and entice. Conscientiously, he threw all the hunks of paper into a litter basket but, after adroitly stepping over a messy mound of dog-do, he wondered if it was worth it.

He was tempted to drop into the drugstore and shoot the breeze with his pal Hank Bianco, but he decided he was really more anxious to get back to his place on Riverside Drive and look at the new collection of *Playboy* nudes.

CHAPTER FOUR

⚜ After an interlude of fantasizing about the *Playboy* models, he got all the ingredients ready for the meat loaf they would have that night. When the ground chuck, onions, ketchup, egg and bread crumbs were blended and in the baking dish, he covered it with food wrap and placed it in the refrigerator to bake later.

He knew Denise was expert at changing food into burnt offerings, but he decided to let her make the potatoes and vegetables, and he would do the salad. This major decision out of the way, he perused *Playboy* again.

Horny and annoyed, he glanced through the booklet Lane Peterson had given him. There were lots of pictures of Natasha Tamarova in it, guiding people through exercises Hardy had never seen before. He tossed the booklet aside. That could all wait till Friday.

He pulled out his college yearbook and looked up George Lassiter. Hardy sneered at the picture of a good-looking young man, and remembered how frustrating college and all of his youth had been for him. Life is not simple for a three-hundred-and-twenty-pound fat boy.

There were other faces he remembered. Al Ricci, Marv Leon, who had worked his way through waiting on tables, Ben Alsop. There was a guy Hardy could feel for. Where Hardy was fat and unwanted, Ben was skinny and pimply and unwanted. Hardy sublimated with food and books, Ben with photography and crossword puzzles. He wondered what had happened to all of them. Hardy had been thumbing through the book at random. Coming across his own face was enough to make him close it and put it away.

When Denise arrived, she found him on the floor, looking through a bunch of old 78 records.

She was all excited about her audition. "It's for Young Sally, in *Follies*. If I get it, we rehearse two weeks, and then play for a six-week stock tour in the Southwest. Pat, this one I'm going to get."

She poured herself a drink and tried to calm down. Hardy had annoyed her by not showing enough interest. He was involved in his silly old records.

He stood up with a stack of records in his hands. "Wait till you hear these."

She sat there, steaming at his reaction to her news, while he got lost in fake memories, listening to Doris Day and "Canadian Capers," Ted Heath and "Peg O' My Heart Mambo," Kay Starr and "Side by Side," Red Buttons and "Strange Things Are Happening," the Ames Brothers and "The Naughty Lady of Shady Lane" and Eddie Fisher, and Henry Rene and the Orchestra, and Perry Como, and Glenn Miller and . . .

Denise could stand it no longer. Close to tears, she got up and went for her coat, yelling, "Patrick Hardy, you are the most insensitive bastard I have ever met."

Hardy leaped to his feet. "I don't understand. What the hell did I do wrong?"

She was putting her coat on and he was taking it off.

"Son of a bitch," she said. "You know how much a job like this means to me, and there you sit, playing those stupid records."

"I'm sorry, baby," he said, kissing her and fondling her body. "I was kind of caught up in my own thing." He kissed her and pressed his body close to hers.

"Quit it," she said. "Getting laid does not

solve every problem. I hate to use what you would call a cliché, but I am not a sex object."

"Of course you are. So am I—sometimes."

"Thanks for that qualification. Well, now does not happen to be one of those sometimes."

They talked for a while and both calmed down, and he listened to her story about the job and very sincerely hoped she would get it—but not for the same reasons she wanted it. Denise was starting to close in and, for Patrick Hardy, that was a bit of a drag.

They were very friendly while they both prepared dinner and listened to the rest of the 78's he had pulled out.

After dinner, they silently watched tv and then went to bed. Their lovemaking was frenetic and climactic, but Hardy fell asleep frustrated, and was sure Denise felt the same way.

She went home that morning, and Hardy spent the rest of the week alone with Holmes, except for Thursday, when Laura came to clean up. Hardy greeted the housekeeper and dutifully chatted with her for a while, but as soon as she turned on her first soap opera, he took Holmes and escaped into the park until he was sure that Laura was through for the day.

That night, he called Denise and reaffirmed their date for the jazz concert the following night.

She seemed fairly chipper. "Great. Do you want me to meet you there?"

"Don't be silly. We'll have dinner first. I'll take you to that place we went to on our first date, Nero's."

"Okay," and she sounded in even greater spirits. "Do you know who's on the bill at the concert?"

He chuckled. "No. You tell me."

"It's The World's Greatest Jazz Band."

"What's their name?"

"You idiot," she said. "That is their name. Some jazz buff you are."

"All I know are Louis Armstrong and Jack Teagarden."

He was being sarcastic, but Denise ignored him. "This is Yank Lawson and Bob Haggart's band. Wait till you hear Bob Wilber on clarinet and soprano sax."

Hardy kept teasing. "I had sax with a soprano once. She was much better than . . ."

"Stop being so silly," Denise said.

"Okay. I'll pick you up a little after five-thirty."

"Okay."

The next day, Hardy showed up at the studio at four, to have his first session with Natasha Tamarova. He had opted for shorts and a tee shirt.

"Please, Mr. Hardy, over here, on the mat."

The woman guided his legs as he first pushed in and out with them, and then lifted up and down.

"You are in fairly good condition, so things won't be too difficult for you. Maybe we'll help you get rid of the little tire around your waist as we fix the leg."

Hardy hated all references to his weight. He restrained the flare-up that was inside him, and said, "Well, I work out a lot, and Dr. Nesor taught me how to do knee shrugs."

"Knee shrugs?"

"Yes," he said, and showed her how he had learned to make his bad knee shrug up and down.

"That is a quadricep exercise, and you are doing it wrong," said Natasha. "But I shall show you how to do it right."

The rest of the session went pretty much the same way. Natasha, the authoritarian, showing and explaining and demanding that things be done exactly and correctly the first time and every time. Hardy could see that he was going to have to balance his need for a healthy knee against his need for keeping his blood pressure down. Next time he came, he would take a tranquilizer.

He finished his workout, but had to wait for the dressing room because it was occupied by a female. He went to the cubbyhole of an office to pick up his card case, watch and money clip.

"Enjoy your indoctrination?" asked Faith.

"Yeah, it was swell." He wanted to keep the

conversation going, but Natasha kept her girls hopping.

Hardy arranged with Lane to have his next session on Tuesday, at the same time. As she turned to mark it on the wall chart, he watched the view of her stretching body with much pleasure. He walked back to the dressing room and wondered which one of those two girls should be his first try. The dressing room was free now.

He turned the dial to "Male" and went in. He had brought a change of underwear and a toilet kit. After shoving his things into his assigned locker, he used the shower and got himself ready for his date with Denise.

Another man came in as he was leaving. They nodded as they passed, and Hardy went out. He glanced at the staircase near the dressing room and wondered where it led. Thoughts of going all the way down ten flights of stairs and finding a locked door at the end, made him walk back to the front staircase and the slow elevator.

He took a cab to Denise's place and arrived at twenty to six. She was ready and waiting. They kissed hello and he admired how well she looked.

"You're not so bad, yourself," and they kissed again.

Downstairs, he found another cab, and they rode up to the West Forties while Denise talked about her prospects of getting the job she had auditioned for.

The driver let them off directly in front of the restaurant. The maitre d' had a table for them as soon as they got upstairs. After they ordered their drinks, Denise said she had to go and call her service to see if any message had come in.

While she was gone, Hardy sipped his scotch and indulged in some mixed memories of the people he had met here. Norse and Hyde. Norse was dead. Hardy was glad of that. Hyde was still awaiting a trial at which Hardy would have to testify. He wished Hyde were dead, too. Price, and Thorp—and Susannah Dow. Christ, did he remember Susannah Dow. He was concentrating on the time they had gotten together at her hotel suite, when Denise came back. She was bubbling with excitement.

"I got it! I got the job! I have to leave Sunday."

A marvelous feeling of joy for the girl and relief for himself came over Patrick Hardy. "That's wonderful. That's great."

He kissed her heartily, and called the waiter over. "Let's celebrate."

"Yes, sir," said the waiter. "You wish to order?"

"A bottle of Dom Perignon, '59, and two steaks." Hardy looked at Denise, who was nodding happily. He continued with the order.

"Hers rare and mine medium. Home fries. And a large salad with Roquefort dressing. Later, you can bring us coffee and show us the pastry tray."

While they were sipping their champagne, she explained that the plane was leaving Sunday. "Could you drive me to the airport?"

"*Certainement*," he said, with his bad French accent.

They laughed, and ate and drank their way through dinner, and then went on to the concert.

Hardy was a different kind of music listener than Denise was. He liked to sit there with his eyes closed and just go with the sound, while she watched everything and applauded at every new riff.

By the time the band took off on "Sweet Georgia Brown," Denise was going crazy, and so was the rest of the audience. It wasn't till the second half of the bill, when they tore it up with "Lover Come Back to Me," that Hardy got out of his self-indulgent pattern and screamed and applauded with the rest.

They rode home in the cab, high from champagne and jazz.

Their lovemaking was the best it had ever been, and Hardy wondered if he wasn't going to miss this girl more than he cared to admit.

Saturday, she went home to pack, and they didn't see each other again until that evening, when he brought her bags to his place and they spent their last night together.

This time, when they made it, it was more or less something they thought they had to do and, as he drifted off to sleep, Hardy reconsidered his wonderment of the night before and attributed it to the booze and the music.

In the morning they had poached eggs and ham, and then he drove her to the airport.

The talk was desultory and meaningless. As she was about to board, Denise said, "I guess this is more than good-bye—it's good-bye."

He was uncomfortable. "Come on, Den; you'll call me when you get back."

"Not while I'm gone, though, huh? Take care." And she walked to the plane without turning around.

"So long," he said to her back.

It had definitely been a farewell with finality to it.

Relieved, he got behind the wheel of his VW and drove home and ate a very large lunch.

On Tuesday at four, when he showed up for his second session at Natasha's studio, he was very pleased to see that he was in Faith Cade's charge. She gave him the same orders and instructions that Natasha had but, coming from Faith, they weren't as hard to take.

"Have you ever been a dancer, Mr. Hardy?"

"No. Call me Pat."

"That's surprising. Your leg turn-out is very

good, for a non-dancer. Keep the knee straight, but don't lock it. That's it. We're finished here, now let's go over to the *barre*."

The girl was pleasant during the session, but Hardy could tell that something was bugging her. Even so, by the time the session was over, he did convince her to have dinner with him that night.

He was washed up and out by five-fifteen, but she wasn't finished until six, so he wandered around Grand Central Terminal and enjoyed himself watching the lemmings, all heading for their own particular trips to their own particular seas.

In the bar, as he sipped his scotch and she her whiskey sour, Faith still looked a little down.

"Come on, what is it?" he finally asked. "Is the prospect of spending the evening with me that depressing?"

"It's not you, but maybe we'd better forget it. I'm afraid I'm not very good company."

Hardy looked at that long blonde hair and those shining teeth. He was not about to let this one get away.

"Come on. What's it all about? Maybe Dr. Sigmund Hardy can solve your problems," and he launched into a comic Dutch patter. "Vas you dere, Hardy? Vot do you know about the girl's problem?"

She tried to grin, but only barely made it.

"It's this part I was up for. I was so sure I had it. Did you ever see *Follies*?"

He nodded and his brow wrinkled up. He was fairly certain what she was going to say next.

"Friday, when I saw you, was the final audition. I was up for Sally, one of the young girls in *Follies*. The short and sad is, I didn't get it. Six weeks in a musical. Instead, I'll have to stay in Natasha's salt mines."

Hardy didn't even try to consider the irony of it all. He just accepted it. He was sorry for Faith—no, he wasn't. If she had gotten the part that would have meant that Denise would still be in New York and Faith would not. He liked the present *status quo*.

"I'm sorry you lost the part, but moping about it isn't going to help. What you need to do is have a good time. What would you like to do? Come on. If you were feeling a little better and wanted to go someplace, where would it be?"

"Well," and her face seemed a little brighter, "I love jazz. I play a little piano," she admitted shyly.

Even as he knew where they were going that night, and even as he considered the second irony, Hardy threw her the straight line to the corny old joke. "You play a little piano, eh? How little?"

She held her hands in front of her, about four inches apart. "This little." She laughed.

"There," said Hardy, "you're better already. Where would you like to go?"

"The World's Greatest Jazz Band is wrapping up their second week here before they leave town. I'd love to go there."

"Done. There's a French restaurant right here in the neighborhood. We'll eat, and then go catch come sound—people still use that expression, don't they?"

"Sure. Why not?"

Dinner was light and breezy, and the girl seemed to be coming out of her doldrums.

He was able to buy tickets to the concert, and ended up sitting not far from where he and Denise had been, only nights before.

This time, a bass-and-drums duet by Bob Haggart and Gus Johnson, Jr., of "The Big Noise From Winnetka" was the smash of the evening.

Her apartment was a cute little place in the Twenties, near Gramercy Park. They had to go through one building and a yard to get to her building, and then up four flights before they reached her one-room-with-skylight.

Faith mixed up a batch of whiskey sours, and they sat and drank, and she talked. "My folks were both in the business. My father played piano in a jazz band. Nothing like those guys we saw tonight. My mother was an actress. She never did much either. I'm supposed to save the family name and tradition, but that's all right, I want to. I dig it. I dig it all. By the way, real name is Cadenski. Do I look Jewish? Who cares? I dig it all, even waiting for my chance at Natasha's. It's like, if that's what my script is, that's the way I'll play it. What do you do?"

"I'm sort of an investigator," Hardy answered, evasively.

"Oh," said Faith, not really paying attention. She replaced the Artie Shaw they had been listening to with several Dorsey LPs. "A little Tommy, a little Jimmy, a little you and a little me. Dance with me."

He got up and put his arms around her, and they stood almost stationary in the center of the room, keeping time to the music with their bodies.

Faith's form felt good next to his. Before he could make his first move, her tongue darted in his ear. Then, as their pelvises worked against each other, she moved her head so that their lips could touch and their tongues could get acquainted.

By silent, mutual accord they stopped, and they began removing their own clothing, watching each other as they did.

Full, round breasts that hung ever so slightly from their weight. Soft, velvety skin without a mark, and wisps of blonde pubic hair.

They kissed again, their hands frantic to touch everything. He could taste the whiskey in her mouth and it was good. It was all good.

When he opened his eyes, he was curled up on the floor and she was sipping a drink and changing the records again.

She smiled at him and walked to the small bathroom, to let the tub fill. He loved watching her going, and he loved watching her coming. Their second coupling was on the couch, and was slower, a tender exploration of what they needed from each other, not like the animalistic attack they had made upon each other the first time.

Now, they did get up and dance. After a while, she went in to take her bath, and he lit a cigarette. After three puffs, he snuffed it out and decided to join her.

She cautioned him as he climbed in. "Steady, no tidal waves, it's a small tub. We'll drown the people downstairs."

Once in, he noticed the same lemon shampoo on the ledge that he had at home. Impulsively, as if he had to perform a necessary part of a ritual, he squirted shampoo on Faith's head just as Denise had done to him.

"What are you doing, you maniac?"

With some, or little, or no pangs of being a heel, he told her about Linda Lee, a Chinese girl he used to know. He lied, and attributed the hair washing to her. "She told me that in

China, lovers always wash their sweethearts' hair."

As Faith joined in the spirit of the thing, and they washed each other's hair, he thought about how he had combined Denny with Linda—but Linda was when he knew the Duchess, the other blonde, the one with the blue monocle. But that was once upon a time, long ago, and in a different country. Besides, the bitch was dead. They were both dead, the Duchess and Linda Lee. They were all dead, the Duchess, and Linda, and Peg and Kate. Was Denny dead? No. Was Pat drunk? Yes.

Somehow, they crawled out of the tub and into bed. The room spun, and spun, and spun until he slept.

He was in a morgue, and all the bodies of the women he had known who were now dead, were on their slabs, row on row. When he awoke, his head was splitting. The noon sun shining through the skylight glared at him. He looked at his watch. Then he looked at Faith, her hair wrapped in a towel, and her splendid, nude body lying there in all its glory. The sight of her made him feel just a little bit better.

Regretfully, he woke her. "Hey, I'm sorry, but I think I made you miss work."

"Don't worry about it," she mumbled. "Wednesday's my day off. We only work four days a . . ." and she rolled over and went back to sleep. This view was nice, too. He watched it for a while and then he, too, went back to sleep.

Holmes. What a bastard he was. In all the years Hardy had owned him, not once had he ever let the animal miss a meal because of his own nightly prowlings. He got up and got dressed and left a note, and went home as quickly as possible.

If the poodle had any rancor for Hardy, he didn't show it at all. He just acted glad to see him, and danced around as his master prepared his food.

Later, Hardy called Faith and explained in more detail why he had left so abruptly.

"That's all right. I like that. Some people would let the dog wait while they got in some more sleep. Do me a favor, please. I like you, and I expect we'll see each other again, but please don't let on when you're at the studio. It would make my life very complicated."

"It's a deal. How's your head?"

"Terrible, in more ways than one. The drinks gave me a headache, but you and your crazy shampooing—it took me over an hour to get all the tangles out. You're crazy, but you're nice. The way I feel, I wish I could take tomorrow off, too."

"How come you only work four days a week?"

"That's Natasha's idea. The way she has us scheduled, she gets a full staff five days a week, and only pays us for four days a week each.

Clever people, these Russians. Some of us take a full day off, but others take two half-days, like Lane. You've met her, haven't you?"

"Yes," he said.

"Well, she takes two half-days off, Monday morning and Friday afternoon. That way, she gets a long weekend. It's all there, on the schedule on the wall in the office, if you're interested."

"I'm not."

"Sorry. Didn't mean to bore you."

"Don't worry, you couldn't."

"Flatterer. Look, I've got to run. I've got all sorts of things that I was supposed to do today, but something or other stole all my time away. Tomorrow, I'm having dinner with an agent-type fellow, Sandy Josephs, and——"

"Hey, hey, hey," he interrupted. "You don't have to report to me."

"How do you like that? I was, wasn't I? I wonder what that means?"

Hardy was sort of puffed up about the whole thing, and very complimented. "See you Friday, at the studio."

"Friday. In case you haven't noticed, I like you a lot, Patrick Hardy."

CHAPTER FIVE

※ His time went its normal way. Despite the fact that he was going to Natasha's twice a week, he still tried to get in a morning workout once a day. Trouble Limited even made some money.

On Thursday, Hardy was hired to find a stray cat. With the help of a few local kids, he managed the job in less than three hours. Minus expenses he incurred paying the kids, Hardy managed to clear forty-five dollars. After he had returned the cat, he wondered if he had paid the kids a finder's fee or a ransom. If the animal was ever missing again, and the same kids found him, he would know for sure.

Some detective, he thought to himself, and mixed curry powder into sour cream to go with the shrimp he was having for lunch.

Meal over, he walked Holmes and bought the afternoon paper. It was Friday, and the phone hadn't rung all day. Neither a client, nor Faith, nor anyone.

It was nearing three-thirty. He remembered to take the tranquilizer he had promised himself, and left to take the bus to Natasha's. After going out and securing all the locks, he decided he didn't want to spend the bus ride without something to read, and since he had read the paper and was too lazy to walk over to Broadway for a magazine, he undid all the locks and went back in. He tried not to listen to Holmes' welcoming bark. "I haven't left yet," Hardy said, as he grabbed a book at random from the shelf and ran out again. The poodle's bark became more strident with disappointment.

The bus ride was enhanced by his accidental choice of reading material. Tommy Hambledon was one of Hardy's favorite detectives. He had read *A Drink to Yesterday* over a dozen times, and would probably read it a dozen times more. Regretfully, he closed the book and got off the bus to go for his therapy session.

Jackson Butler opened the dressing room door while Hardy was getting dressed. The slight man peered cautiously into the room, and only when he saw Hardy did he enter.

"I'm always afraid I'll startle some woman in her . . ."

The man didn't finish the sentence. He and

Hardy got into their outfits, trading conversational inanities and monosyllables.

He's as fast as a rabbit, too, thought Hardy, as he went to the mirror for a final look, and took a drink from the water fountain. The thought came when Hardy saw Butler scooting out to the studio before him, even though he had come in afterwards. This thought led Hardy to, yes, he does remind me of a rabbit, the hurrying rabbit in *Alice in Wonderland*. Rabbits are noted for their great sex life. Sex. Faith. And by that time, Hardy was in the studio himself, and talking to the final object of his thoughts.

"Good afternoon, Mr. Hardy."

"Good afternoon, Miss——" and he peered at her nameplate, "——Miss Cade."

She suppressed a smile, and they started to work. Hardy had been lifting weights and working out for years, but the exercises during these therapy sessions made him use muscles he didn't even know he had.

"Relax, Mr. Hardy, you're too tense. If you're tense, you can't do the exercise properly."

"I wonder why I'm so tense?" he whispered teasingly to Faith.

"Quiet. Less talk, more work." This was from Natasha.

The phone rang, and Natasha's commissar-like tones were heard again.

"Hello. No, Mr. Miklos, I do not know where Lane went after she left here."

Two exercises and ten minutes later, the phone rang again. One of the other instructors answered it.

"Who is it, Carmen?" Natasha demanded.

"It's Frank Miklos again."

"Hang up," the Russian woman said testily. "Tell that young man to stop calling, or Lane Peterson will never show her face here again."

While this was going on, Hardy and Faith made grimacing comments on Natasha's behavior, and he told her to call him at home when she got through. By this time, Natasha had turned and was looking in their direction. Like two kindergarten children caught in mischief, they industriously went on with the current exercise.

Hardy had finished for the day and was slowly heading for the dressing room. Mr. Butler was right behind him. The phone rang again. Faith made the mistake of answering it.

There was blood in Natasha's eye as she asked, "Who is it?" Faith didn't answer. She merely nodded.

"Hang up!" Natasha screamed. "This is a place of business, not a lonely hearts club."

Hardy and Butler exchanged glances and entered the dressing room. Butler sat down, exhausted. Hardy imagined the man to be in his fifties. He forgot about Butler and worked at divesting himself of his very sweaty tee shirt. As he did, he wondered about Lane Peterson and her boy friend. He didn't blame Miklos for worrying about her. Hardy was happy about the thing he had going with Faith Cade, but he couldn't help wondering if he could score with Lane Peterson, too.

Once out of his wet clothes, Hardy considered taking a shower, but settled for a wash at the sink, instead. Butler was starting to get himself together.

"They do wonders for my back, but after all these years of sitting at a desk, it's hard work."

"What do you do?" Hardy asked politely, as he dried his armpits and chest.

"I have a small travel agency. As soon as I get the strength to get up, I'll give you one of my cards."

Seeing that the man was making light of it, Hardy laughed and put on a fresh tee shirt.

Washed, talcumed and almost fully dressed, the detective went into the bathroom to get a tissue to blow his nose. Later, he could never explain his actions, not even to himself, but for some reason, he opened the shower curtain.

And when he did that, he solved the problem forever of whether he could get Lane Peterson into bed. Nobody ever would again. Her gaping eyes and protruding tongue almost made him gag. Mesmerized, Hardy stared at her nude body, suspended by a towel tied to the shower at one end and to her neck at the other. She was quite dead.

"Here's my card, Mr. Hardy. Mr. Hardy, what's wrong? Oh, my God!"

Hardy gently shoved Mr. Butler out of the bathroom. The man was staggering from what he had seen. Hardy sat him on a bench and groped in his jacket for his tranquilizers. He took a capsule and asked Mr. Butler if he wanted one.

"No, thank you, I have my own pills. That poor girl. Somebody should call the police."

"I will," said Hardy, as he watched the man take a pill from a small gold box. Butler placed the tiny pill under his tongue and sat there, waiting for it to dissolve.

"Are you all right?"

"I'm fine, Mr. Hardy. Don't worry about me. You do what you have to do."

He was about to, when Natasha pounded on the door. "Gentlemen, please. We have other people waiting to use the dressing room."

Hardy opened the door and asked Natasha to come in. She looked at him curiously.

"It will have to wait for another time, Mr. Hardy, and certainly another place."

He closed the door.

"Mr. Hardy, are you some sort of a madman?"

She irritated him so much that he didn't even

consider trying to tell her gently. "Natasha, Lane Peterson is dead."

The woman didn't bat an eye.

"She is hanging by her neck in the shower."

This got a reaction.

There was almost a perverse satisfaction in Hardy as Natasha stood there, for once without a thing to say, and with a blank expression on her face. However, Natasha's immobility was short-lived. She snapped herself out of it, opened the bathroom door and looked for herself.

He heard the shower curtain being closed, and then Natasha came out and shut the door.

"This is terrible! People will be afraid to come here."

Hardy made an angry noise. "You can brood about that all you want. I'm going to call the police. Don't touch a thing. And you'd better tell everyone who's here not to leave."

The precinct and the homicide cops came, and went into action. Everyone was questioned and names were taken down. Natasha was asked to supply them with a list of all her clients. She refused. "My clients have a right to their privacy."

"For God's sakes, Natasha," said Hardy. "The man's only trying to do his job. Call your lawyer, and if he has any sense, he'll tell you to hand over the list."

The cop nodded thanks to Hardy, and added,

"And a list of the people who work for you. And we especially want to know who came in today, and if you know who any of the girl's friends were."

Natasha stood up, her voice thundering, and brought her lithe reed of a body close to the burly policeman, who was only just a little taller than she. "I'll tell you who did it. It was Frank Miklos, her lover. He called all day, asking for her, but that was only to establish an alibi. He killed her in a jealous rage. He was very possessive of her. Have you ever met him?" She asked the last of Faith, who didn't respond in any way. The girl seemed quite shaken by it all.

"Yes, M'am. Miklos," said the cop. "Is that k-l-o-s?"

"Yes."

"Would you happen to have his address?"

"It's the same as Lane's," Natasha said, evilly. "They were living together. She was keeping him."

The questioning went on, especially of Hardy and Butler, who had found the body.

"Why'd you move the shower curtain? Were you going to take a shower? Did you see something?"

"I honestly can't tell you. I simply opened it."

The cop looked at him quizzically, and then turned to Butler.

When they were finally finished and out on the street, Hardy asked Faith if she was all right.

"I feel scared. Pat, could you come home with me, or take me home with you? I don't want to be alone tonight."

"Sure," he said, his libido reacting despite the situation, and his conscience reacting in annoyance to his libido, but not too much. "What are you afraid of? Do you know something you're not saying?"

"No," said Faith. "It's nothing like that. I'm not afraid of anything in particular. I'm just frightened."

She had calmed down by the time Hardy had fed them all. The two of them were relaxing on the chaise, sipping brandy, while Holmes tried to get his share of both the chaise and the brandy.

"An alcoholic," she laughed.

"Yeah," said Hardy. "Gets it from my side of the family."

Faith was nice and calm, and then the phone rang, and he could feel her clutching up again.

"Hello."

It was Natasha.

"Mr. Hardy, I want you to solve this case for me."

"You've got to be kidding."

"I am not kidding. I was talking to Ward Nesor about the terrible thing that happened, and he told me that you are a private detective. You must take the case and solve it quickly. If it goes on too long, my reputation will be ruined. The way the police go about doing things, by the time they catch the murderer it will be too late, and I will be out of business. By the way, are you coming in on Tuesday, at four?"

He laughed, despite himself. "Yes, I'll be there." He mouthed silently to Faith, "It's Natasha." Back to the phone, "Look Natasha, the police are better equipped, have more facilities . . . uh . . . me . . . uh, knowhow . . . uh, more everything than I do. Why don't you let them do their job, and let me stay out of it? Private detectives should stay out of murder cases. If there's one thing I've learned in this business, it's that."

"No. I will not hear of it. I demand that you take on my case."

It was Natasha, plus the rising cost of living, that raised Hardy's fee. Up until then, he had been getting $100 a day and expenses. "All right," he said, with trepidation, "a hundred and thirty a day, and expenses—and get me a duplicate of all those names the police wanted."

"A hundred and thirty dollars is too much money."

"Take it or leave it," he replied.

"A hundred and twenty a day and expenses—which you will keep to a minimum—and two free sessions a week at the studio for the next year."

Hardy was enjoying this.

"A hundred and thirty a day, take it or leave it."

"I take it."

CHAPTER SIX

⊗ After the phone call, realizing what Hardy did for a living, and learning that he was taking on the case, Faith reverted and became almost a basket case. Hardy gave her several more drinks and put her to bed. He stayed up to watch television and not think of the new problems he had taken on. When was he ever going to learn?

When he got into bed, she seemed a little more peaceful. He kissed her gently on the cheek and fell asleep, almost immediately.

In his sleep, he felt the warm pressure against him. He awoke to find Faith, still sleeping but curled like a ball next to him, her ass pocketed in his loins. Of course, he had erected. He reached for her breast and pulled her closer. Faith, in turn, made mewing noises and pushed herself closer against him. In semi-sleep they made it, and then, still coupled, they fell asleep again, with Hardy more positive than ever that sex was better than any tranquilizer.

Morning.

He had entered her normally, but from the rear, and their sleeping bodies had formed a human layer cake, his hands cupping her breasts, his prone body resting on her back and her left hand caressing his buttock.

He assayed the situation and went back to happy limbo.

They were in the same position when he awoke again. The wonder was that he hadn't crushed her. He gently disentangled himself from the pretzel of their bodies and quietly slipped out of bed. He interrupted his journey to the john to cover her with the floral sheet, pausing long enough to admire the contours of her form. He started to get horny again.

Enough.

No, never enough—but there were things to be done.

Sheet on, journey completed, bladder relieved, he took a shower and started to get dressed. A glance in the mirror at the small spare tire that was forming around his middle made him switch to a sweat suit, and he went into the gym to work out, even though it was Saturday.

He was finishing off on the bike when Faith

wandered in, wearing his robe with the sleeves rolled up.

"Some layout you've got."

The robe wasn't quite secure. "Some layout you've got," said Hardy. And, strangely enough, she blushed and tied it close. She yawned prettily.

"With a setup like this, I don't see why you ever bothered with Natasha."

"The exercises," he said, using the conversation as an excuse to stop peddling. "I needed somebody to show me the proper exercises—or some improper ones."

"Seriously," she said, "with this setup, it would be simpler to have a therapist come to you."

He got off the bike and started toweling his neck. "I thought I already had that."

Faith shook her head and winced. "I drank too much. Look, it's too early in the morning to play word games. What does a girl have to do around here to get a cup of coffee?"

"Coming up." And he made them a breakfast of French cinnamon toast and coffee.

After breakfast, she got dressed and made several phone calls while he took another shower and finished reading his detective book. When he was done, he placed it gently back on the shelf and turned on the tv. Nothing interesting. He turned it off.

"Hey," he yelled at her. "How would you like to have dinner with me?"

"Swell," she said, coming into the room looking a lot better than she had the day before. "I'll cook you one."

Hardy hesitated for a moment. He enjoyed cooking, and he enjoyed eating what he cooked, but he also enjoyed being catered to. "All right. What's it going to be?"

"Let me look and see what you have in the kitchen, and I'll decide then."

He showed her the pantry and where the Deepfreeze was.

"This looks interesting," she said. "Now scoot—and no critics in the kitchen, please."

Faith watched with pleasure as Hardy put away two helpings of her curried lamb. He was nibbling at the remains of the coconut and cashews when she unveiled the chocolate soufflé.

He felt the dessert melting in his mouth and sighed with contentment as she poured him a second cup of coffee. He caressed her leg as she went by.

"Not while I have a hot coffee pot in my hand. God, you have all your appetites working at the same time, don't you?"

Hardy squinted open his eyes and noted that she was pleased by his over-all reaction. He managed to rouse himself from the table to get the brandy. It wasn't often that he bothered with the balloon glasses, but the meal and the girl warranted it.

He warmed the glass in his hands and sniffed the contents. He sipped, savored the taste and swallowed.

Faith looked at him in wonder. "You are about the most complete sensualist I have ever met."

"For that acute observation and remark, and for that meal, and for your beautiful body—and because I am a modern man and you are obviously a modern woman, I must add for your brilliant mind and talents, because you are a person and not only a sex object, I hereby formally ask you to marry me."

"You idiot," she laughed, and drank her brandy.

Hardy lit a cigarette to cover his confusion. He was glad she had assumed it was a joke. What scared him was that he knew he had meant it. Heaven help him, he was in love with this girl. He had liked all the others, and one, a stripper, Ruby Red, made him passionate whenever he had only a passing thought about her. But this one, wonderful to look at, wonderful to talk to, wonderful in the kitchen, wonderful in the bedroom—who could ask for any more? He could. In love or not, he was not ready to get married, now or ever. Never. Thank God, she had thought he was joking.

They made love after dinner.

"I'm not staying tonight, Pat. Besides having nothing to wear, if I do stay, I won't get a thing done tomorrow, and the weekend is the only chance I have to catch up."

He nodded, and offered to take her home.

"Don't be silly, just put me in a cab. I may not have acted it last night, but I'm a big girl and I can take care of myself."

When he returned, carrying the Sunday papers, he set them aside and tried to evaluate the situation—his and Faith's, not Lane Peterson's death. After a confused while, he found it simpler to put his mind to the detective problem rather than the personal one. Both were going to be hard nuts to crack.

Monday morning, just as he was starting to make breakfast, the doorbell rang. On cue, Holmes started barking. Hardy told him to be quiet, and checked to see who it was through the closed-circuit tv. It was a messenger.

"Yes," he said, through the intercom.

"Package for Patrick Hardy."

He went out and received it—*it* being the papers he had asked Natasha to supply. He was surprised that she would spend the money to have it delivered, considering that he was going to be at the studio the next day.

"She must really be anxious," he said to Holmes.

Holmes had no comment.

Hardy usually tacked all pertinent data

concerning a case to the cork wall next to his desk, but the bulk in his hands was ridiculous. He shoved it into a drawer, and went back to making breakfast.

As he ate, he knew without even looking through the bunch of names that Frank Miklos was probably the best bet, but that he would have to wait until the police were not all over Lane's boyfriend like a blanket.

Hardy scraped the dishes clean and put them into the dishwasher, then went back to his desk to note Miklos' address and phone number.

His phone rang. It was his friend of Manhattan North, Detective Gerald Friday.

"Hi, Gerry, how are you?"

"Don't give me that crap. I understand you just happened to be in the area of another homicide yesterday. What is it with you? Are you some sort of Typhoid Mary, or do you go looking for trouble?"

"Trouble Limited, that's my name."

"If that's supposed to be funny, Pat, it's not." He spoke the next very slowly and precisely. "You are not going to get involved any further in this case. I am correct in making that statement, am I not?"

"Sorry, Gerry, I already am involved."

"All right, you were there, you were a witness—but that ends it, understand?"

"Sorry again. The lady who owns the studio hired me. I told her she should let you people handle it but she insisted, and a guy's got to make a buck. I'm on the case."

The policeman sounded annoyed and disgusted. "With your brand of luck, you'll probably stumble over the solution after a bunch of working stiff cops break their collective humps doing the work and putting the pieces together. You'll trip over your own feet into the tail end and figure it out. What bugs me is that I know it's going to happen. It's happened like that before, and it can happen again. What also bugs me is that nobody will ever mention those cops, but I can just hear it about you, the private detective."

Friday's voice went up a notch in a mocking imitation of a Park Avenue rich bitch. "Isn't that Patrick Hardy wonderful? He solved it all by himself." His voice was in its own vocal range now, but still angry. "Shit!"

Hardy was silent for a second, making sure that Friday wasn't going to go on. "Gee, Gerry, it was nice of you to call me up for this nice friendly chat."

"Balls!" And he hung up.

Hardy went back to the envelope Natasha had sent, and wrote down the information on Frank Miklos and pinned that to the cork wall. That done, he was sitting and wondering what to do next when the doorbell rang again. He ignored Holmes' noisemaking and checked the outside tv. He saw a familiar, ugly but good-looking face on a solid, six-foot-two frame that didn't have an ounce of fat on it. It was Steve Macker.

"Steve. How are you? Wait a minute, and I'll come out and let you in."

Holmes barked even louder as he excitedly chased Hardy down the hall. The two friends greeted each other and then, as Hardy led the way back into the apartment, Holmes and Macker said hello.

Inside, Macker poured himself a shot of I. W. Harper and examined Hardy's private tv system.

"What's with all this hardware? It's like trying to get into Xanadu. Who do you think you are, Citizen Kane?"

The remark gave Hardy's mind something to conjure with. Friday had compared him to Typhoid Mary, and now he was Citizen Kane. He was coming up in the world.

He answered, "No, just like to keep my privacy. I didn't notice your bike. You leave it on the Coast?"

Macker took a hearty swallow. "Yeah, in pieces. Lost an argument with an oil slick on the road. But I walked away, and that's what counts. Got into skydiving while I was out there. Boy, that's a kick. You ought to try it."

Hardy shook his head. Macker would jump out of a plane or cross the street with the same aplomb.

"No, thank you. You got anything lined up?"

This time it was Macker who shook his head.

"If you're interested," said Hardy, as he unpinned the slip with the particulars of Frank Miklos on it, "you could check this fellow out for me. He lives on Great Jones Street, downtown."

Macker took the piece of paper and shoved it into his pocket. "First thing in the morning. Meanwhile, I know a place that has the best scampi in the world. It's a bar in Brooklyn. They also have a pool table. I'm going to spot you thirty points for who buys dinner and drinks, and a ten dollar side bet, just to make life interesting."

Hardy knew he was being hustled, but went along with the suggestion anyway.

"Sounds fine. What time do you want to go?"

"I'll be back about six. I've got some unpacking to do and a few phone calls to make. Don't worry if I'm a little late, I might get lucky."

"In that case," said Hardy, "you'll never show up at all."

"Might be. Might be. What do you hear from Ruby?"

"She's in Europe. Paris, I think. Ought to be home any week now."

"Good. See you later."

When his friend was gone, Hardy went back to his office to try to get some work accomplished. His first job was to get Macker's glass away from Holmes. After a little argument, which Hardy won, he gave the dog a biscuit as a peace offering. Then he rewrote the information on Frank Miklos and pinned the new sheet on the wall.

His next step was to pull out the list of names and figure which ones the police would work on first. It seemed logical that, after questioning Miklos, the police would first talk to the girls who worked for Natasha, then the clients who had been there that day and finally, the other clients on the list.

This meant that Hardy's best bet, if he didn't want to be bumping into police everywhere along the way, was to start backwards and visit the clients who had not been there. It would probably be a waste of time, but at least the traffic would be light.

The trouble was that that list had more than 200 people on it. He hadn't the slightest clue as to which one he should see first. So much for reverse logic.

He'd let Macker find out about Miklos, and tomorrow, when he went for his session, he would go early and question the girls who worked for Natasha. That settled, he went into the kitchen to make lunch.

He was preparing a salad. Holmes was way off in the bedroom, sleeping. No sooner had

Hardy started scraping the carrot, than Holmes came strolling in.

"How do you always know?" Hardy chuckled and gave the poodle a chunk of carrot to chew on.

After lunch, they went out for a walk and a paper.

The newspaper story on the murder gave him no new information. When he finished reading it, he tossed it into the basket under his desk and looked longingly at the chaise and then at the barber chair that stood near his desk.

To get some energy flowing, he got up and went to the phonograph. Denise had given him a five-record album of songs from Broadway shows. He had never played it. He put them on.

He listened to Merman and Mary Martin and all the rest, and never thought of Denise at all. Macker's question about Ruby had set him thinking about the stripper, though. He shifted his thoughts to finding a book to read while he waited until Macker got back.

Stranger in a Strange Land—that was a good book. Hardy enjoyed reading books over and over again. He took this one to the barber chair and settled in.

It was seven o'clock when Macker's ringing awakened him. Hardy let his friend in, grumbled about being hungry, washed his face and fed the dog.

Macker wanted Hardy to take his VW, but

Hardy had it safely tucked away in the garage. Besides, he knew that a night out with Macker would mean that neither of them would be in any shape to drive, but Macker would want to anyway.

"Okay," said Macker, who was a little high already. "Subway or cab?"

"I'm too hungry to wait out a subway ride. Let's get a cab."

Macker laughed. "I'll make a deal with you. If the first cab you get agrees to take us to Brooklyn, I'll pay for the ride."

Macker paid for the ride.

Hardy was feeling good already. The cab let them off on Pacific Street, and they were walking to the bar. Macker was bitching. "Of all the cabs, you have to get one whose garage is in Brooklyn and just brought a fare into Manhattan. Wait till I get you in that game. I'm going to cream you."

Lou's was a neighborhood bar and restaurant where the locals ate and drank. Macker introduced Hardy to Lou, a big, healthy sort of a guy who looked like he might have been a boxer at one time but had quit while he was ahead.

"First one's on the house. Haven't seen you in a long time, Steve. What have you been doing with yourself?"

"Been out to Hollywood. Worked in a few pictures."

"No kidding," said Lou. "Tell me the names, and I'll take the wife and go see them."

"I'll let you know when they come out," said Macker. "I've been bragging to Pat about your scampi. How about it?"

"Sure thing. Coming right up."

They ate a lot and drank a lot and played pool a lot. At first, Hardy shot over his head and made runs of ten or more each time he shot, but eventually Macker wore him down and beat him for twenty dollars and the tab for the evening.

Three locals came over and started coming on like hustlers. Neither Hardy nor Macker was interested. They tried to walk away from it. They said good night to Lou and went outside, either to round up a cab or take the subway home.

The three from the bar weren't far behind. When they called out, "Hey, you punks," Macker turned, ready and happy.

Hardy, who usually found ways of avoiding situations such as this, was too drunk to be his normal, scared self. He, too, turned as the three attacked.

Hardy knew Macker was dealing with two of them. He, himself, felt his opponent's hand graze his chin. This annoyed him, so he grabbed at the arm that powered the offending fist and broke it. He left the man on the ground and turned to help Macker, but by this time Lou had rushed out of the bar, and he and Macker had the situation well in hand. Seeing this, Hardy sat down next to the man with the broken arm and passed out.

CHAPTER SEVEN

❈ His mouth felt like a million soldiers with dirty boots had marched through it. His head felt like those same soldiers were there now, double-timing and using his skull for bayonet practice from the inside.

Slowly, Hardy opened his eyes. The place looked familiar. If it would only stop spinning around, he could identify it.

"Welcome to the world. Come on, grab your socks. Up and at 'em."

That was Macker. If he had the strength, he would gladly kill him.

"Hold it down to a roar, Steve, at least until . . ." He didn't say another word. Luckily, he had finally identified the location as Steve Macker's apartment on Eighty-First Street, and knew where the bathroom was. When he came out, he felt a little better, but not much.

Later, as they both held the black coffee Steve's friend had made, and were sipping and staring at each other, Hardy said, "Who's she?"

"I'm not too sure," said Macker. "Some sort of a humanitarian. She showed up after we had that little mix-up and you passed out. I had a few drinks with her and she offered to take us home. I'm not sure, but I think I have a new roommate."

Hardy peered at the woman and discerned that she was no more than thirty, very pretty and very well put together.

"I must really be hung," said Hardy. "That's a very good-looking woman, and she doesn't turn me on at all."

"Thank you—I think," she said, and refilled their cups. "I'm Irene, and you're Pat, and he's Steve."

"Thanks for getting that all straightened out for me," Hardy muttered. "I don't think I could have managed it by myself."

Macker was walking around and, as usual, was coming back faster than Hardy ever did from one of their joint meanderings.

"When am I ever going to learn? My mother warned me to stay away from bad company."

Macker laughed at Hardy's complaint. It was his usual one, and he was used to it. "Relax, Pat. In a year or two, you'll feel fine. Lou said not to worry about that guy whose arm you broke.

His friends took him over to the hospital, and he's going to be fine."

"I broke somebody's arm?" He felt sick all over again, but this time he controlled himself and didn't have to do any running.

Macker sidled over to him. "Pat, do you think you can get home by yourself? I mean now. I sort of would like to get acquainted with Irene."

Hardy groaned. "You have no soul."

"I know, but I have something else."

"Funny. Funny. Can't say I blame you. If I were feeling half human, I'd be thinking of the same thing. Oh, my head! How you can even think about it is beyond me."

"Clean living, my friend, clean living."

Hardy curled his lip in the nastiest look he could manage. "I'm going home to sleep this off. I don't know why I'm even thinking of this, or why I should even mention it, but if you can squeeze it in, you might check out that guy. You remember, I gave you his name and address."

Macker grinned and pulled the slip of paper out from somewhere. "Frank Miklos, Great Jones Street. It will be the second or third item on my agenda for today."

Hardy marveled at his friend. He would have shaken his head if he hadn't thought that it might fall off.

"Do that, my obnoxious one, and you're on salary as of right now. Have fun with . . . ?"

"Irene. Her name is Irene. See you later, pal."

Somehow, Hardy managed to make the journey to his apartment, and to manipulate the locks and alarms on his door. He crawled to the chaise in his office, where he collapsed. Holmes, who had already taken possession, grudgingly moved to a nearby corner. Hardy patted him gratefully and fell asleep.

Sometime around two in the afternoon, he awoke with no hangover at all and a ravenous appetite. He gobbled down a piece of bread and butter and a glass of milk, and then soaked under the shower. When he came out, he shaved. The razor hurt when he scraped over the spot where he had been clipped, but that seemed to be the only damage.

He made a lunch out of cold cuts and cheese and went out. Amazed at his own recovery, he gave a passing, envious thought to Macker, and tried to remember what the hell had happened. It was all a blank, and that worried him. Then, as he approached Broadway, it came back. The memory of the occurrence worried him even more. He resolved then and there never to go out carousing with Macker again. Even as he thought it, he knew he wouldn't live up to it.

The paper he bought didn't have anything new on Lane Peterson's death. He put it aside and looked at the people sitting around him on the subway. They were the usual people—reading or staring or talking to each other or themselves. One trio attracted his attention. At first, he thought they were all together, but then he realized the girl was a stranger to the older woman and the teenage boy. The woman and the boy were seated on either side of the girl and were having an animated conversation across, over and around her. The girl was tickled by the whole thing and was trying not to break up. Hardy would have liked to stay and watch the outcome, but the train stopped at Forty-Second Street, and he had to switch to the shuttle.

At the studio, Hardy tried to question the girls on the go, but Natasha kept shunting them back to the clients, and what little he did get was next to useless.

Natasha's back was turned. "Faith, where's that other one? I saw her on Friday."

"You mean Carmen?"

He nodded.

"Carmen Ramos. Today is her day off. She'll be in tomorrow—or you can see her Friday, when you come for your next session."

"Right. What are you doing tonight?"

"I'm sort of tied up." She smiled, and he managed not to grin back like an idiot. "I'm not doing anything tomorrow. Call me tomorrow, in the afternoon. It's my day off, remember?"

"Mr. Hardy. It is almost time for your session. Don't you think you should get dressed?"

Hardy nodded at Natasha but did not salute.

Jackson Butler came in at that moment, and they walked together to the dressing room.

"How are you feeling today, Mr. Butler?"

"Very well, thank you. Yourself?"

"Fine. I mean, the other day, when we found the body, you looked sort of shaken by it. Does it bother you to be using this room?"

"Of course it bothers me, young man. I am not a stone. The trick is not to let it affect me. My heart is not as good as it should be. She was a nice girl. So pretty. Twisted values. But it's a shame she had to die so young."

Hardy stopped undressing. "I beg your pardon?"

"What?"

"You said, 'twisted values.' What did you mean by that?"

Mr. Butler smiled tiredly. "Just a generalization. All the youngsters today, such twisted values. Well, I am ready to meet the Mad Russian." He closed his locker and left the room.

Hardy became very pensive as he finished getting ready, but when the thoughts had finished caroming around his brain, he wasn't really sure what they had been all about. He made a mental shrug and joined the others.

It was he who was to meet the Mad Russian.

Natasha was working with him today, personally. Suddenly, his hangover came back and he remembered that he had neglected to take a tranquilizer.

"Please, Mr. Hardy, you are fighting me. Less thinking. Don't use your mind, use your body. If you analyze it, it will disappear. Don't bother to answer. Breathe and bend. Breathe and bend. Better. Better. Very good. Come over here."

She led him to the mat and gave him a two pound weight to strap around his left foot. He was very familiar with the weight. He had used it before, in his own program of exercises. He had also used it in a manner it hadn't been designed for. The image of the weight, covered with blood, and another image of Terry Hyde leaning over to kill him, were so vivid that he almost thought they were real. The next image was Terry Hyde's shattered face. The sequence was wrong, but the memory was right.

"Mr. Hardy, are you feeling well?"

"Fine, Natasha, fine. Got a little dizzy from all that breathing. Guess I hyperventilated, or something."

"Well, your hour is almost up, anyway. Relax here for a while before you go back to the dressing room. You did very well. It would be better if you didn't think so much, but very good. In a short time, that quadricep will develop. Enough talk. You are not my only client." She walked away and came back immediately. "Are you making any progress? I mean, with the investigation."

"A little, Natasha, a little."

She said nothing and walked away again.

As he lay there, Hardy thought about what he knew, which was not much. Lane Peterson had finished work for the day on Friday, at noon. Everybody believed that she had changed clothes and gone out. Obviously, she had not. She was killed sometime between noon and five o'clock, when he and Butler had found her. All the clients that morning had been elderly fat ladies. Lane's boyfriend, Frank Miklos, was a very possessive type. The killer must have come from the outside and sneaked up those back stairs.

Hardy sat up with a start. "I never knew that," he said out loud.

"What?" Natasha demanded.

"Nothing," said Hardy, as he played with the brand new thought that had popped into his head. The back stairs. He would have to check them out. The night before, and the work-out he had just finished, did not make that particularly appealing, but it should be done.

He stretched and went to the dressing room. His partner in torturedom was waiting for him. They talked about nothing in particular for a while, and then Butler said, "Young man, I know in today's day and age, when one male asks another male to join him for dinner, it is usually assumed to be a homosexual overture. In my case, I assure you, it is not. I just find you a most interesting person, and fine myself without plans for this evening. Would you care to join me for dinner?"

He hadn't wanted to cook, anyway, and it gave him a great excuse not to go traipsing down those ten flights of stairs. Besides, he liked Jackson Butler. "Mr. Butler, it would be my pleasure."

He didn't know why, but he was surprised to find that a mild man like Butler would go in for hot Mexican food. It was a very expensive place in the East Thirties that Hardy had once been to with his own travel agent. He wondered if it was an "in" place for those in the business.

After the margaritas, which Hardy doubly enjoyed because he usually stayed away from salt, which was bad for his high blood pressure, they ordered.

By the time they had finished all the *seviche*, and the *tostada*s with cheese, and the pork in chili sauce, and half the pitcher of *sangria*, Hardy loosened his belt and asked if Butler would mind if he lit a cigarette.

"Not at all. My doctor has ordered me to quit, but I would enjoy the aroma."

Hardy nodded. "My doctor has ordered me to

quit, too, but I'm afraid I don't have your will power."

A section of Hardy's mind listened with amazement at Butler's remark and his own response. My God, thought the section, I sound like an old man sitting in a rest home for invalids.

He smoked while the older man philosophized on the younger generation and their twisted values, pretty much echoing what he had said earlier, in the dressing room. Hardy nodded politely, without bothering either to argue or agree.

Outside, Butler offered to drop him off.

"No, thanks. I think I'll walk for a while. Some thinking I should do."

"All right, but be careful," Butler warned. "Nowadays, it isn't safe on the streets. These youngsters with their twisted values would just as soon steal a penny from a dead man's eyes. Be careful that one of them doesn't hit you on the head for what's in your pocket."

Hardy nodded absent-mindedly while Butler harped on. He flagged a cab for him, and lit a new cigarette as he watched it drive away.

Some thought was trying to surface. It was tugging away at the dense layers that covered it. He walked on and on, hoping that the thought would come by itself, just as the one about the staircase had. Annoyed, he flagged his own cab and went home.

After feeding Holmes, he wrote down the

conclusions he had come to in the studio and pinned them to the cork wall. That done, he called his service. No messages. He guessed Macker had never gotten beyond item one on his agenda.

He lit a new cigarette. Damn! He was smoking too much.

He put it out, but several minutes later lit another one, poured himself a brandy and turned on the tv.

The credits had just finished rolling, and he recognized the music. Hardy made a joyful noise and curled up on the chaise, welcoming Holmes, who had come to join him and perhaps steal some brandy. The picture was *Singing in the Rain*, one of Hardy's favorites.

CHAPTER EIGHT

⚜ The next day, Macker showed up, smiling like the proverbial possum. Hardy never did know what that expression meant exactly, but in Macker's case it seemed to fit.

As he drank his coffee, Macker beamed and silently bragged about his new friend, Irene.

"That good, huh?"

"Sorry," said Macker, "I don't get your drift."

"Shut up," said Hardy, "I suppose you didn't get a chance to check Frank Miklos out."

"Yes, I did. If I'm given a job to do, I deliver. You ready to hear my report?"

"Wait a minute." He dialed Faith's number. Her sleepy hello made him want to forget everything but her. "Hi, it's me, Pat. Need some company?"

"What a coincidence," she teased coquettishly. "Here I am in bed, trying to decide what to do with the rest of my day."

"I've just decided for you." He looked over at Macker like an adolescent showing off his new bike. "You stay in bed and keep it warm. I'll be over as soon as I can." And he gently cradled the phone and kissed it.

"Hey," said Macker. "Don't you want to hear my report on that Miklos kid?"

"Yeah, but make it fast, will you. I've got things to do today."

"Investigating the case, right?"

"Right," said Hardy, and they both laughed.

"All kidding aside, Steve—what did you find out?"

"Miklos and the girl had been living together for almost a year. It's his place, a loft. He claims to be a painter, but besides the money she brought in, he picks up spare cash hustling a little pot and a few pills. I'm not sure whether he's into any heavy stuff. I didn't want to come on too strong. If you're acting like a guy looking to make a light connection for some grass or uppers, it's not too cool to switch around and start shopping for heroin—at least, not the first time down. You want me to keep digging?"

"Yeah," said Hardy. "See what else you——" He stopped in mid-sentence, then said, almost rhetorically, "I guess Frank Miklos is what you might call a youngster with twisted values."

Macker looked strangely at his friend, but he was used to Hardy's aberrations, and finished his coffee and left without another word.

The cab driver who ferried Hardy to Faith's apartment was certainly against type. The man wore a good straw hat and a Brooks Brothers suit with a rep tie, and smoked his cigarette with a holder. He looked very posh and somewhat Franklin D. Roosevelt. Hardy appreciated the fact of it, and leaned back to enjoy the ride.

In a frenzy of accumulated passion, Faith and he fell into bed immediately after she had let him in.

Amidst it all, he said, "I've been thinking about this all morning."

"I've been thinking about it all week," she answered.

She was sleeping now, and he was sitting up on one elbow, smoking a cigarette and staring at her. It was not just his usual fondness for voyeurism. Patrick Hardy was in love.

When she started to come awake, he very guiltily squashed out the cigarette and pretended to be dozing. She kissed him. Her lips were warm and moist and made him think of the first girl he had ever kissed.

He wanted to say so many things, but he guarded against them all. While she fixed them a snack, he rambled on about the case—anything but say what he wanted to.

"Hon?"

"Yes, Pat."

"Those back stairs by the dressing room—can they be used? I mean, is the door open when you get downstairs?"

"Oh, sure. I use it all the time. I can't stand waiting for that pokey elevator, and I don't mind all the flights. That day I met you in the drugstore, that first day?"

He nodded.

"You left before I did, but I used those back stairs. I think we reached the street at the same time. At least, we went into the drugstore at the same time."

"Yeah, that's right. What about Carmen? Did she know Lane pretty well?"

"I think so. Both of them were working for Natasha when I started. They seemed to be friendly with each other, but I don't know if that was just at the studio or outside, too."

God, how he wanted to tell her! "Another thing—the second time I was at the studio, the day Lane was killed—because of all those phone calls, I knew about Frank Miklos. Was that usual? I mean, the phone calls? or was it just that day?"

"Just that day."

"Then, everyone didn't know about him being Lane's boy friend?"

"No. Some of the girls maybe, but none of the customers." She walked over to him and kissed the bruise on his face.

"You really are the detective today. Is that how you got that?" She kissed it again and sat next to him.

His emotions were in turmoil. It seemed that at any moment his knees would begin to shake, and his insides felt the way they usually did when he was driving very fast.

"Faith—I love you."

"You know how I feel about you," she answered.

"No. I don't mean for a few weeks, or a few months. I love you—I want to marry you."

She stood up. "That's very sweet. I don't know what to say. It's a very nice compliment. I think I love you, too, but it's been so quick, it's hard to say. I've been in love before, and it's exactly what you said—sometimes a few weeks, sometimes a few months——"

When she paused, he started talking again. "That's the way it's always been for me, too, but this is different. When I first realized it, I was afraid of it, afraid of being locked up for life."

She wandered around the small apartment, lighting a cigarette and taking long puffs into her lungs. "The trouble is, Pat, I'm still afraid of being locked up. I know other men. I go out with other men. In fact, there's one man, in particular, I see quite a lot. I've been to bed with him. I like him. I like you. I like the life I lead. And I'm ambitious. I want to be an actress. Marriage would only get in my way."

Hardy sat there, not believing a word she said. He knew that, eventually, she would marry him.

"We can still go on seeing each other—you know, for our own kind of therapy. I'm not just saying this to salve your ego, but no man has ever excited me, or made love to me, the way you do."

He sat there. For the first time in his male life, the shoe was on the other foot. He had no way to deal with it emotionally at all. "Would you write that up and have it notarized, please? I'm sorry, I didn't mean that. A joke. A very bad joke. Look honey, why don't you think about what I said? I'd better get up and get out. I've got work to do, and I'm afraid I've been sleeping on the job. Another joke, I think."

They looked at each other silently, and she started putting the dishes in the sink. Hardy got dressed and left.

He waited just outside her door, hoping that perhaps she would run after him, or call his name. He put his ear to the door. If he could hear her crying? He thought he heard her clearing her throat, but that was all he heard.

What a fool he'd been. But that was neither here nor there. Neither was the case he was supposed to be working on. He thought about going down to Great Jones Street. Instead, he took a cab home and went to sleep.

It was a simple dream. Just he and Faith walking through fields of flowers in slow motion, like all those terrible deodorant commercials he hated. The dream camera separated them and zoomed to a Dali-like shot of a tree branch, which looked like a shower head. Lane Peterson's body was dangling from it, hanging on a twisted towel. There was printing on the towel. The camera went in closer. Printed on the twisted towel was the word *values*. The announcer said, "Buy values today, twisted or untwisted."

He was back in the morgue that he had seen in another dream, the morgue with all the bodies of the women he had known who were now dead. They weren't on slabs this time. They were all neatly filed away in filing cabinets, and on each cabinet was a neatly printed card: *values*.

Hardy awoke, sweating a great deal. He went to the john and washed the sweat and odor away. It was about three in the morning. Holmes joined him in the kitchen and watched while Hardy cut a hunk of salami and a large piece of bread, and opened a fresh bag of potato chips and a coke. Hardy wasn't sharing any, so the dog lay at his feet, waiting for the crumbs that would come his way. Part way through his repast, Hardy placed a stack table next to the barber chair in his office and set up his victuals there. Holmes followed while Hardy browsed through his collection of Mark Twain and pulled out *Tom Sawyer Abroad* and *The Man That Corrupted Hadleyburg.*

Laura found him sleeping in the chair when she came in later in the morning.

He greeted her grumpily, chomped up two Gelusil tablets and washed them down with a glass of water, and went to the bedroom to try to get back to sleep.

No hope. No way.

He got dressed and was on his way out, when he said, "Laura, why is it that every time you leave, I can't find anything in the kitchen? Then by the time I get it all straightened out, it's Thursday again. Like the bread knife. You keep hiding it. Last week, I finally found it behind the mixmaster."

"Of course," she answered, not at all perturbed.

"Why of course?"

"If it's back there, you won't cut yourself."

He threw his hands in the air at her logic. "Okay, Laura—" and before he could get out the words, "I'm leaving," Holmes started barking. He stared mutely at Laura and the dog, and left.

He bought the paper and threw it away without reading it. He went to a movie and left after fifteen minutes. Despite Laura and her soap operas, he went back to the apartment.

She was through in his office. He sat there at his desk and sulked. He thought about calling Faith, but she wasn't at home. He could call the studio on the pretense of reporting to Natasha, in the hope that Faith would answer the phone. But what if Natasha answered?

His phone rang. Hardy picked it up eagerly.

"Hi, Pat. Steve."

"Oh. Hello, Steve."

"What's the matter?"

"Nothing. You find out anything more on that Miklos kid?"

"Just a few nibbles, but I think I'll have to play it cool for a while. Let me give it a few more days."

"All right."

"But that's not why I called. I was looking through the paper, and there's a horse named Patrick Hardy running today. If you get over to the OTB on 72nd Street, you can still get a bet down."

"That it?"

"Yeah, later." And he hung up.

For want of anything better to do, Hardy did just as Macker had suggested. He went over to the Off Track Betting office and bet ten to win and ten to place. Then he went several blocks further downtown to the Baskin Robbins ice cream store and bought himself a french vanilla cone. By the time he had finished the ice cream and walked back to the betting parlor, the race was over. Patrick Hardy had come in dead last.

CHAPTER NINE

⚜ On Friday he got to the studio early again. This time it was not to interrogate the girls but to talk to Faith. As he left the elevator, he was annoyed to see her at the foot of the single flight of stairs, talking to a sharply dressed, good-looking young man with black hair and a Ryan O'Neil face.

For a fraction of a second, Faith seemed to be uncomfortable. She overcame it and said, "Hello Pat, I'd like you to meet my friend and my agent, Sandy Josephs. Sandy, this is Pat Hardy. He's the private detective who's investigating Lane Peterson's murder."

The two men eyed each other carefully and shook hands.

He's gay, thought Hardy, but knew immediately that he was wrong. This was probably the other guy she had told him about, and Faith, being Faith, had probably told Josephs about him. Hellos went along with the handshakes, and Hardy went on up to the studio. He saw that Carmen was there, and asked Natasha if he could talk to her for a few moments.

"All right, but not too long. I have a business to run here."

Carmen said she hadn't known Lane, outside of work. Hardy, still suffering over his present situation, made a tentative pass as a form of revenge on Faith. "I get good vibes from you. Do you think you and I could ever get together?"

Carmen tilted her head and looked amused. He wondered if she knew about him and Faith. She said, "That depends."

Hardy put on a fake scowl. "Is that a yes or a no?"

"If you're not too impatient, I might get more definite—one way or the other." And she looked back at him over her shoulder as she went back to work.

He wondered if Carmen knew more than she was saying about Lane Peterson. Then he wondered if he wasn't merely inventing that, merely to have an excuse to see her. If his first wonder was correct, perhaps the best thing to do would be to double-date with Faith and Carmen and Steve Macker. It might mend things with Faith, too, and he was sure that Macker would not object. Carmen Ramos was a very good-looking woman.

Hardy considered Macker and his situation with Irene. He went to the pay phone and called him.

"Steve, this is Pat. By the way, you're some handicapper."

"Sorry, pal, can't win 'em all."

"Anything new?"

"Nope."

"What's with you and that Irene female?"

"Gone. A real mystery lady. I woke up this morning and she was gone. A real, long, dramatic, romantic note about ships that pass in the night and all that crap. I'll let you read it sometime."

"No, thanks. Look, there's a girl who works here that might know something, and I've been having a thing with one of the other girls here. How about if we all went out together? We might find out something."

Macker snorted. "Are you trying to stick me with a dog, just because I gave you a loser at the track?"

"No, Steve. This one's a knockout. Even if nothing comes of it as far as the case goes, she can be my personal contribution to your private life."

"All right. Let's do something tonight. But I'm warning you——"

"Such an untrusting fellow," Hardy said, and hung up the phone.

"You're late, Mr. Hardy." That was Natasha.

He glanced at his watch and went double-time to the dressing room. Mr. Butler was just leaving, and they nodded hello. When Hardy changed and returned to the studio, he found that he was to work with Faith. He controlled hinself and said nothing, concentrating fully on the exercises.

"Very good today, Pat. The leg is really coming along, but you're going at it as if you're mad at the world. Is part of that meant for me?"

"Of course not, I'm just a compulsive. How about dinner tonight?"

"I don't know, I was planning——"

"Let's make it double." He pretended to look around and think. "Why don't you ask Carmen? I think she'd like my friend Steve."

Faith hesitated, thinking it over. The vote was yes. On the pretense of getting some equipment, she went over to Carmen and asked her. Carmen looked at Hardy in a funny manner, then nodded her head.

When Faith came back, he was smiling. She smiled back. "It's a date."

"Fine," he said. "Do you want to leave from here, or are you going home first?"

"Here will be fine."

"Mr. Hardy, during this hour we work, we do not talk." Natasha again.

Pat crossed his eyes at Faith, which made her laugh, and she nearly choked stifling it. Things were going to be all right, all the way around. He finished his workout with a greater burst of energy than he had even had before, but this time there was no anger behind it, only hope.

As usual, he and Jackson Butler had their little chat while they washed up and dressed. The damaged pipes in the women's dressing room had been repaired, so the men's place was now back to being strictly a male domain, and they didn't have to rush in and out as they had been doing. Butler seemed more relaxed because of it.

"Besides the terrible thing that happened to that poor girl," he said, "I was always worried that I would walk in on a naked lady. What would I say to her?"

Hardy chuckled. Butler was obviously distressed at the thought of such a situation. Hardy privately considered what he would do in the same setup. It was an interesting mini-fantasy.

Butler was finished before him, but the man wouldn't leave. He kept fussing with his tie or making another remark, as if he were waiting so that he and Hardy could leave together. Normally, Hardy didn't mind Butler. He was a nice enough character. But he wanted to think about

HUNG UP TO DIE

the case, and about dinner. When he was finished getting washed and dressed, he very deliberately sat down and lit a cigarette. At last, Butler seemed to get the hint. "Good-bye then, Mr. Hardy, until Tuesday."

"So long." And he got lost in the pleasure of his cigarette and his reveries. His thoughts were pleasant enough, but when he began to light a new cigarette, they led him to the back stairs, just outside the door.

Abruptly, he stood up and strode out of the dressing room, past the closet, and started down the ten flights. At the door, he had a different thought and turned back. Glancing around to see that no one was in sight, he went to the closet and opened it.

The shelves contained towels, soap and other supplies. It was not a large closet. Hardy stepped inside and closed the door behind him, to see if he could. He could.

Satisfied with this new revelation, he was about to leave when he stepped on something. He knelt down. It was only a bar of soap. He was picking it up to put it back on the shelf when he noticed the tiny patch of white powder. If it hadn't been directly under the cake of soap, he would never have seen it at all.

It was probably only some spilled cleansing powder. Playing detective, Hardy undid the paper on the bar of soap and used the outer wrapper as a container to hold the grains of whatever it was he had found on the floor. Using his finger, he swept his find onto the square of paper, folded it up and put it into his pocket. Feeling very professional, he left the closet and resumed his journey to the staircase.

The ten flights were well lit and clean, and the door was not locked. He was breathing heavily when he opened it. Not much, but enough to annoy him.

By some circuitous twisting and turning of the stairs, he found that he was only a mere twenty feet from the elevator. He walked towards it, only to see the doors open and Mr. Butler emerge.

The older man looked at him as if he were an apparition. "For heaven's sake, Mr. Hardy! How did you manage to get down before I did?"

"I—uh—tried the stairs."

"Good for you. I had to wait almost twenty minutes for that silly elevator. It must have gotten stuck. I wish I could manage to walk all those steps. Good-bye again."

The private detective chewed his lip and watched Butler disappear into the mass of people that came and went in the terminal. He was lighting his second cigarette when Macker showed.

They nodded to each other, and Macker stopped Hardy's hand as he was returning his cigarettes to their resting place and took one out for himself.

"Got a match?" Macker asked.

Hardy smirked before he answered. He wondered why Macker's presence always made him feel like he was back in the army, always prompting him to answer with army-cliché retorts. "How about a kick in the ass, so you can get it started?"

Hardy didn't know if Macker's look of distaste was for his comment, or the cigarette smoke he was breathing in. He never did get to find out. At that moment, the door that Hardy had used burst open, and Carmen and Faith appeared, breathless and laughing.

Macker's expression changed to one of delight. "I don't know which one you think is yours, but the one with the black hair is mine."

Hardy's face took on a similar appearance as he replied, "Whatever you say, Steve." He introduced Macker to the girls and the girls to Macker.

Carmen seemed just as pleased with the arrangment as Macker was, and Faith was smiling at Hardy, and Hardy, at her.

The happy quartet first went across the street for a few drinks. While they drank they argued food and restaurants. Hardy wasn't that crazy about Japanese food, but he was too content to dispute it. Besides, it was three against one.

Squatting wasn't as bothersome to his knee as he thought it might be, and the tempura and saki were better than he had expected.

Carmen and Macker were getting along very well together. Now that his operative was zeroing in on his assignment, Hardy gave his full attention to Faith, which she had been getting all along anyway.

"Happy, baby?"

"Of course," the blonde answered, her eyes dancing. "I'm always happy."

And then the first part of the evening was over. Macker and Carmen in a cab going to his place or hers, and Hardy and Faith in another cab going their own way—specifically, Faith's apartment.

He had just turned for a second to make sure that the door was secured for the night, when Faith had his jacket off. She was ruining a perfectly good tie in her efforts to remove it from his neck. "Come on," she said, "strip for action."

She assumed a karate stance, looking very good for a person who had just drunk as much saki as she had. "Time for combat. Didn't know I was trained in karate, did you? Actress has to know everything. Come on, attack."

And he did. And they made love right there on the floor, as they had done on a previous occasion, only this time they didn't bother to take their clothes off.

"No fair," she murmured happily. "You caught me when I wasn't looking. Let's make it seven out of eight falls." And she finished undressing him, stopping to kiss and caress along the way.

Hardy reciprocated.

As much as he tried, they never did manage those eight falls Faith had insisted on.

CHAPTER TEN

⚜ In the morning, Hardy made no mention of love, but Faith was glowing through her hangover, and he was sure that things were going to go his way.

"I'm beat, Pat. Do a girl a favor and get out of here, before we start touching each other again. If that happens, I'll never get anything done."

Somehow, his clothes had been picked up and hung in the closet. They both made the mistake of going to the closet together and, in the interval between she buttoning her blouse and he tying his tie, he started unbuttoning her blouse and searching out what was underneath.

They were naked again. As they thrashed around the couch, twisting and hugging and pushing and grinding and kissing and whispering and moaning and whimpering and creating their own roller-coaster, he heard her say, "Oh, Pat, I love you! I do love you."

When he awoke, she was staring at him. "You!" she said. "Go to the bathroom, wash up and get out. I'm not coming out from under this sheet until you're gone."

He did as he was told.

At the door, he called out, "Faith, I'm leaving."

"Good!" was her muffled answer.

He opened the door.

"Pat."

He turned in the doorway. Faith was sitting up, the sheet clutched to her chin.

"Yes, hon?"

"Pat, don't you dare come near me—I just wanted to look at you before you left. Damn, we are good together, aren't we?"

He nodded and blew her a kiss and left, closing the door firmly behind him.

He and Holmes spent the weekend together, with television and the Sunday papers. He never heard from Macker, nor had he expected to.

Monday morning, Hardy was ready to go. Still no Macker. He called his home but no answer. He thought of calling Carmen Ramos' home but decided against it. He called Faith's number and then hung up in mid-ring, remembering that she would be at work. He chuckled as he wondered if Carmen would be, too.

Itching to do something, he found himself looking up Sandy Josephs' number and address. The agent had an office in midtown. Hardy got dressed and went to see him.

As he told the receptionist his name, he wondered what he was doing there. When he was taken into Sandy Josephs' office, the agent wondered the same thing, and asked, "Well, Mr. Hardy—what can I do for you?"

Hardy knew he was there to gloat at the competition, but he couldn't tell Josephs that.

"It's about Lane Peterson," Hardy invented. "Like most of the girls working for Natasha, she was an actress—or at least, trying to be one. Did you ever have any dealings with her?"

"As a matter of fact, I sent Lane out on several calls. She wasn't signed to us the way Faith Cade is, but we were thinking about it. She didn't get any of the jobs she was sent out on, but she seemed to have a sort of animal excitement. We figured if that girl ever got the right part, she might zoom way up there. Your instincts are very good, Mr. Hardy. If she had lived, we might have been calling Lane in this week and discussing the prospects of signing her with us. I can give you her picture and resumé, but beyond that, I'm afraid that's all I can tell you."

Hardy passed the manilla envelope with Lane

Peterson's picture in it from hand to hand as he rode down to the lobby of Sandy Josephs' building. The thought that he had lucked into something was very strong, but he simply couldn't put his finger on what it was.

He stopped at a pay phone to call his service. Steve Macker had called only minutes before. The message was for Hardy to meet Macker at the Broadway and Lafayette Street stop on the Independent subway, as soon as possible.

"Is that it?" Hardy asked the service operator.

"No, there's more," she answered. "Nicholas looks like he's splitting."

"Sweetheart, could that be Miklos instead of Nicholas?"

"Yes, that's it."

"Thanks." And he hung up the phone and looked for the fastest way downtown.

"What the hell kept you?" said Macker, as he led the way. "A girl was up to see him about half an hour ago, and she came down with some canvases and a suitcase. He was still inside. It was a toss-up whether to follow her or stay. I decided to stay. That's when I called you and left word on your service."

They were just outside the building now. Macker was still talking. "A few minutes ago he came out with a small bag. Just then a police car came cruising by, and he scooted back inside. I don't know if the cops are keeping tabs on him, or if it could have been just a coincidence. They're not anywhere around now."

Hardy sent his eyes up and down the street to check Macker's statement.

"That kid is ready to go. There's only the door—no fire escape from his windows. Do we go up after him, or what?"

Hardy shrugged. "Let's go."

"Soft or hard?" asked Macker, and then answered his own question. "I say hard."

Hardy nodded and then followed him up the several flights of stairs.

Macker kicked in the flimsy door and they both stood to the side.

After a few seconds, Hardy dropped to the floor and peeked in. The thin young man with the long hair was standing in the middle of the room, holding a jacket in his hand, but poised and ready for whatever. Hardy had only seen his face that one day, but he assumed it was Frank Miklos.

Hardy and Macker were in the room. Despite the open windows, it was stiflingly hot.

"Going some place, Miklos?" Macker asked.

The boy said nothing. He just watched and waited.

Macker said, "You relax by the door, Pat. No sense both of us going after one skinny kid."

Carelessly, Macker went after the youngster. When he made his move, he got the surprise of his life. He grabbed at Frank Miklos and came up with nothing but the jacket. Miklos had evaded his grasp and was behind him. Macker turned quickly, dropping the jacket, but the boy wasn't attacking, only evading. Miklos took a quick look to see what Hardy was doing.

"Don't worry, sonny," said Macker, very much annoyed at himself. "It's just you and me. Stay out of this, Pat."

Hardy was very content to do just that.

The young man was in the center of the room. Hardy was behind him at the door and Macker was in front of him, directly in front of one of the windows.

"Come on, kid. Make life simple for yourself. We're not here to hurt you. We just want to ask you a few questions."

Suddenly Miklos turned, as if to try for Hardy and the door, and just as suddenly he turned back and leaped over Macker's head. Using the window sill and his first jump as a propellent, he went out the window and spanned the open space to the fire escape across the way.

Barely catching the metal rail, the boy hung on and swung to and fro, and then pulled himself up. He spent only a second to look at the two men and make a classic gesture with his middle finger, and then he was crawling through a window and was gone.

"A Goddamned acrobat," said Macker, adding all the curse words he knew, as he and Hardy scrambled down the stairs in pursuit.

By the time they reached the street and checked out the other building, Frank Miklos was gone.

Back in the apartment, Hardy looked around. Except for a mattress and several torn canvases and the jacket on the floor, the loft was empty. Hardy picked up the jacket. The strange feel of it made him heft it for a second, then he found the source of the weight in the inside pocket.

The thick brown paper envelope contained six little books, 3½ by 6 inches, with the seal of the United States on them.

Hardy thumbed through each passport, complete in every detail except for the bearer's picture. He looked at the different names and statistics and official-looking stamps and perforated numbers. Several were even stamped to show entry and exit to and from different countries.

As he examined them in concentrated amazement, Hardy lit a cigarette. He felt Macker taking the pack, but his mind was involved with the six little books.

"So that's what this is all about," said Hardy. "Fake passport racket. Well, what do you know? You want to see these, Steve? They're real works of art."

Macker was pacing back and forth in the loft, puffing away at his cigarette. "Who the hell would figure he would try a stunt like that? A stunt man wouldn't try a stunt like that—be too smart."

Macker was looking out the window now, gauging the distance and looking as if he wanted to try it himself, just to see if he could do it. "Anything. I was expecting anything. A punch. A kick. But to jump out the stupid window. Lousy kid. Goddamned acrobat!"

Hardy laughed, but not too loud. He really didn't want Macker venting his anger on him.

"Come on, Steve, let's get out of here. I'll buy you a drink."

"You know," said Macker, "it's really not that hard. I could do it."

"Steve, you interested in that drink?"

"Yeah," he said, trailing behind Hardy, but he kept turning back and looking wistfully at the window.

CHAPTER ELEVEN

⊗ Macker and Holmes were off in a corner, with Macker doing in what was left of a bottle of I.W. Harper and Holmes trying to help him. Hardy was at his desk with two envelopes, the one with Lane Peterson's picture in it and the more important one with the six very good forged passports.

Hardy searched for a cigarette. He remembered where they were and retrieved them from Macker, who was now smiling. "Got to hand it to that kid. Sure took a lot of nerve to pull a stunt like that."

"I agree," said Hardy. "But it's the other stunt he was trying that I'm interested in."

"What's that?"

"Okay," said Hardy. "Try this one for size. Someone at Natasha's studio is in the passport racket. The obvious choice is Butler, because he's in the travel agency business, but we'll see. Lane Peterson either found or stole these six passports in the dressing room. She told the owner of them that she had them but was willing to sell them back. That was probably the boy friend's idea. The owner of the passports agreed, but instead, sneaked into the dressing room and killed her, thinking she was in it alone. He never knew about Frank Miklos, at least not until the last few days, when Miklos got in touch with him to start bargaining all over again. That's why Miklos was moving out—going underground to safer quarters until the deal could be completed."

"Good," said Macker, "And he has even more bargaining power because not only does he have the passports, he knows who killed Lane."

"Right," said Hardy. "Sounds like the sentimental type. But now he's up a tree. He hasn't got the passports any more. He is a very definite liability. I'll give you a brand new job. Watch Mr. Jackson Butler. What do you want?"

"Huh?"

"What shift do you want?"

Macker scratched his head. "Eight to four. I hate to think what that's going to do to my beauty sleep, but it's better than giving up my love life."

Hardy dialed a number from his book and got Jose Hernandez on the line. "Hello, Mr.

Hernandez, it's Patrick Hardy. You remember me? You helped me out on the Kate Arnheim case."

"Sure I remember you. You have another case where you need someone to talk Spanish?"

"No. Just a straight surveillance job. I've got one man for the eight to four, I need two other men. Can you help me out?"

"Sure. I'm glad you called. Business is sort of slow these days. I'll take one shift, and my brother Manny can take the other."

Hardy and Hernandez talked about money and the other particulars of the job. When they were through, Hardy hung up the phone and poured himself a drink of Cutty Sark.

"How come so conscientious?" asked Macker. "You only used me for a part-time watch dog over the kid. What's with the full-time bit with Butler?"

Hardy savored the scotch. "With Miklos, all we had was a suspect. I think with Butler, what we have is a murderer. Nice little guy, too. Sure could have fooled me."

"What if he is fooling you now? What if you've picked the wrong man?"

"Thanks, Steve. I needed that. Give a guy confidence. Well then, I'll just be spreading a little of Natasha's money around. All of you guys come under the heading of expenses."

Hardy wandered about the apartment.

Macker had a nice glow on. "Why don't you settle some place? Something bothering you?"

Hardy nodded. "We didn't tell—excuse me, didn't mean to incriminate you—I didn't tell the cops about what happened today at Miklos' loft. I really should tell them about the passports and Butler, and I think I found something in a closet at the studio. Maybe the best thing for me to do would be to call——"

The phone rang.

Hardy picked it up.

It was Detective Gerald Friday. Friday began blistering away, without even letting Hardy say hello.

"Damn your stupid, silly ass, you, you, you ... moronic ... private detective!" The policeman virtually yelled the last two words. "How many times do I have to tell you to stay out of official police business? What the hell were you and that other one doing on Great Jones Street today? Who do you think you are? I'll tell you who you are! You are one of the stupidest bastards it has ever been my misfortune to know. Ever since that first day on the Dorothy Robbins case, when you started haunting me, I should have known. My phones have been ringing all day about you. Right now, we could arrest you for breaking and entering, aiding and abetting——"

"Aiding and abetting what?" Hardy tried to say.

Macker looked, on hearing the phone crackle and getting the attitude, if not the sense, of the tirade. He turned away and poured himself another drink.

Hardy was not that fortunate. Friday was still going non-stop.

"Yes, aiding and abetting. We had that kid covered. He's probably the one who killed his girl friend, and if you hadn't gone in and played Hollywood hero, we'd have him now."

"Wait a minute," said Hardy. "If you had him covered, how come you didn't catch him when he came out of the other building?"

Friday made a noise and hung up.

Hardy felt a little better—not much, but a little. The source of Friday's steam was not only Patrick Hardy. Obviously, some policemen had not been paying enough attention to their job. He gave Macker the gist of what it had been all about.

"You going to call him back and tell him what you have?"

Hardy sat and thought. Meanwhile, Holmes padded over from Macker to Hardy, looking for a more diligent ear-scratcher.

"Screw him," said Hardy, "Hollywood hero. Let him do his own leg work. Good night, Steve. I've got some thinking to do, and you've got to get up early tomorrow morning."

"Don't mind me." Macker drained his drink, stole another of Hardy's cigarettes and left, with Holmes hearalding the departure to all those in earshot.

Hardy put all the bolts into place and went back to his office, where he placed the fake passports in the wall safe behind the George Grosz drawing.

He tossed Lane Peterson's picture in the drawer, along with the bulky envelope he had first received from Natasha. He started to remove the Frank Miklos information from the cork wall, but his hand stopped in mid-motion and just dropped.

Hardy was tired. He picked up his drink to finish it, changed his mind, and poured it down the drain. He was glad that Macker wasn't here to see that.

He dreamed that night. In the morning, when he awoke, he couldn't remember any part of it, but he knew there had been a dream. And there was something about it that it made him so shaky that he took a tranquilizer before he even got out of bed, even though he knew he was going to take one later, before he went to Natasha's.

As he lay there, the phone rang. Despite the tranquilizer, he started nervously at the jangling sound.

It was Western Union.

"Yes, this is Patrick Hardy."

"We have a message for you. The message

reads, 'Ready or not, here comes Mama.' There is no signature."

"Well, could you tell me who sent——?"

Hardy was talking into a dead phone. He sighed. The little green-and-white capsule was starting to take effect. He rolled over and allowed himself to fall back to sleep.

When he awoke again, he had forgotten about the dream and the phone call. The upper thigh muscles of his left leg were killing him. He imagined it was due to the stretching that Natasha had been putting them through.

He went to the john, and then to the kitchen for a glass of grapefruit juice. Then he got dressed for running and went over to the track in Riverside Park to do a few laps. If he was going to work out at all that day, the leg needed to be loosened up and, he thought wryly, so did his mind. The first few times around, he thought only of the effort. Then his legs began looking after themselves and his mind started off on little runs of its own.

When he was done, he felt a lot better. He wasn't any surer of the facts about the case, but his leg felt a lot better and so did he.

After a shower and a late breakfast, he read for a while, then watched television. Macker called him once to say that Butler was in his office and had obviously eaten his lunch in.

"That it?"

"That's it."

Hardy got dressed during the last hour of *That Hamilton Woman*. He was going to skip the tranquilizer and have a leisurely walk downtown, instead. While he watched the movie's progress, he had a peanut butter sandwich and a glass of milk.

He was dressed. He had eaten. He was ready to go.

Hardy moved to turn off the tv and got interested in the final scene after Nelson's death. Though he had seen the picture before and knew how it ended, he had to wait and see the final seconds and hear Vivien Leigh's final words.

That done, he sighed and turned off the set, and wished for falsely remembered yesterdays.

Since he was so early, he wandered for a while. His trip took him to Seventy-Eighth Street and the Museum of Natural History. He recalled going to the Planetarium as a kid. He made a mental note to visit the place when he had the time, and headed for Central Park and downtown.

When he was entering the terminal, Hardy saw Butler ahead of him. He held back when he saw Macker walking away, and almost missed the swarthy man who seemed to be going in the same direction as Butler, but was apparently lost. Hardy watched in appreciation as one of the Hernandez brothers did a very professional job. He and Macker had probably just switched over. At least, that's who he assumed it was—he had never met either one of them.

As Butler waited for the elevator, and as his shadow waited in a corner, Hardy realized that the Hernandez—Jose or Manny—had one of three choices: wait downstairs, and take the chance of losing his subject; or watch what floor the elevator went to and then go to the same floor when the elevator came back, still taking a chance of losing his man; or get on the elevator with the man and become someone he might recognize the next time he turned around.

Hardy watched Hernandez go for choice number three, the choice he would have made. As he waited for the slow-moving car to go up and then come back down to him, he realized that he would have to wrap Butler up fast, or else prepare himself to use new sets of men every few days.

With this new worry to bother him, he rode up to the studio. He tried not to laugh while Hernandez asked the girl in the office a question in Spanish.

Natasha was screaming. "Where's Carmen? That girl is never around when I need her."

Faith nodded at Hardy and answered Natasha's raving. "It's Tuesday. Today's her day off."

"Excuses. All I hear is excuses. You're late,

Mr. Hardy." She then turned to Hernandez and said, in bad Spanish, "*No aqui. No aqui.*"

Hernandez bobbed his head, smiled, and went down the single flight of stairs.

Hardy gave his valuables to the girl inside the small office and went to the dressing room. Butler was suited up and just coming out.

"Hello, Mr. Hardy."

"Mr. Butler."

"Lovely weather, isn't it?"

"Yes, it is," Hardy answered, and went on in. There were two other men using the room. Hardy didn't know them and figured that they were new clients. Manifestly, Lane's death hadn't frightened away business. Another reason to finish up quickly—Natasha might realize that it didn't matter, and fire him.

He sat in his shorts and tried to rethink on Butler. One second he was sure he was right about the man, the next second he was just as positive he was wrong. Such a nice guy. But Hardy knew that some of the nicest people ever had committed murder when they thought they had to.

In the studio he was terribly preoccupied, and did his exercises haphazardly. Natasha's yells brought him out of it. It was only then that he noticed the ring on Faith's finger. He stared at it, and she whispered an answer to his unspoken question. "I've been trying to tell you all session. Sandy gave it to me. We're going to be married before the end of the year."

He said something about the best of luck, and finished his workout in a similarly disjointed manner, but for a different reason.

In the same sort of funk, he left the studio, bought a paper and took the subway home. He read the paper without really absorbing the information. His eyes went to a short item and read:

"The nude body of an unidentified man, shot through the head in the manner of an underworld execution, was discovered in a shallow grave on unused farmland in New Jersey this morning."

Hardy read the words, but the facts didn't, or couldn't, or wouldn't, penetrate his befuddled brain.

In the apartment, he fed Holmes and then, without even bothering to change, went out to the park. The track was closed, so he ran around the footpath that encircled the basketball courts.

When his brain had cleared and he caught himself comparing himself to Tom Courtenay in *Loneliness of the Long Distance Runner*, he sat on a bench and had a breathless laugh on Patrick Hardy.

Hardy looked around. The park was almost empty and there was no one near him. Out loud, he said his favorite quote from Sabatini: "He was born with a gift of laughter and a sense that the world was mad."

Now, as he ambled back to his apartment, he was Scaramouche cum Stewart Granger, loving or leaving women, as the fancy took him.

Inside the apartment, he accepted Holmes' wet greeting gratefully and hunted through the *TV Guide* for the proper escape. None available.

He ate leftovers from the refrigerator and combed his bookshelf for his copy of *Scaramouche*. It was only after an hour that he remembered he had never owned it as an adult.

It was the kid, the fat kid, Patrick Hardy, who had owned—stolen from the library and owned—the copy of *Scaramouche*. It was the same kid who, in fear of being found out and sent to jail for theft, burned the book secretly one night in the fireplace, and suffered his mother's questions and his father's piercing eyes because of the awful stench the covers had made in burning.

His lips lifted in a smile that didn't quite make it, and he pushed the memory away. Then he disconnected the bell on the phone, took several tranquilizers, and proceeded to sleep the clock around.

On Wednesday evening, when he awoke, he went to the john and wet his face, and then to the kitchen to put some of Holmes' frozen chuck out to thaw. Then the two of them walked over to Broadway for a paper.

Skimming through the paper, he saw the newest story, the one with more facts. He read the headline as he walked: "SLAIN MAN IDENTIFIED AS FRANK MIKLOS, SUSPECT IN MURDER CASE."

The story went on to describe how the nude body of the young man had been found in a shallow grave in New Jersey the day before:

"Frank Miklos, identified by his fingerprints, was apparently shot at another location and then taken to the New Jersey grave site, where the body was found by Barney Thompson, a retired chicken farmer. Thompson explained that he was walking his dog and that his dog actually dug up the body.

" 'Wasn't much of a grave,' Thompson said, 'The next rain would have washed it away.'

"Thompson, on whose land the body was found, and whose house was only several hundred yards away, remarked that he hadn't heard anything during the night.

" 'The dog barked once or twice,' he explained, 'but I thought he was just being jittery. It's a good thing I didn't go out to see, or I might have been killed by one of those gangster fellows, myself.'

"Thompson, who is 76 and a widower, lives alone."

Miklos had been dead only a short time and,

since the body was nude, his fingerprints had to be checked with Washington before positive identification could be made.

"As well as could be ascertained, the victim had been shot in the head, a sign that could indicate that this was a gangland slaying."

The story had a lot more words in it, but no more information.

Holmes was tugging at his leash. Hardy had been standing stock-still while reading. The dog was anxious to get home and now, so was Hardy.

He called Macker. "You read the paper?"

The actor said he had.

"Butler, or whoever, finally got smart and put out a contract on our young friend. If he had done that in the first place with the girl, he would have been better off—and so would I, for that matter. Steve, forget about the surveillance. It was a waste of time to begin with, and now it's even more so. I'll call Hernandez. Hey, I forgot to ask—did you ever get anything from Carmen?"

Macker snorted. "That information I shall save for when I write my memoirs."

"Oh," said Hardy. "Okay."

He hung up and dialed Hernandez's number.

"Jose, it's me, Pat Hardy. Call it off. It's a bust. I'll pay you as of midnight tonight. Send me the bill."

"Right."

"One thing," said Hardy, before he broke the connection. "Who was that on Butler, right after my man stopped working on Tuesday? Was that you or your brother? Very classy piece of work."

Jose Hernandez laughed. "That was Manny, my kid brother. Some actor, huh? Look, someday, why don't we get together?"

"Sounds good. Maybe a poker game or something. *Adios*."

Hernandez laughed again. "Yeah, sure thing. So long."

That settled, Hardy concentrated on making stuffed peppers and watching television.

The next day he escaped the house before Laura arrived, and went to see three movies in a row.

On Friday he did the same thing, not even bothering to take his four o'clock class with Natasha.

Friday night when he got home, Holmes was barking and the phone was ringing. He told Holmes to shut up and picked up the phone.

"Hello, stud. If there are any broads in the place, throw them out. Tell them you have a new roommate."

"Ruby, when did you get back?"

"You sound surprised, Pat. Didn't you get my telegram? Or is that happiness I hear in your voice? And you'd better say yes."

He remembered the telegram over the phone.

So that's what it was all about. She was still talking.

"I'll be right over. Don't start without me. Hey, I'm in town for only about three weeks, so you have a house guest, if you don't mind me cramping your style for that long. Will it be all right?"

"Just fine with me, Ruby. Just fine."

CHAPTER TWELVE

※ He placed the receiver back in its cradle and was suddenly very hungry.

He went into the pantry and came out with a can of anchovies, a can of boned turkey and, logically enough, a Turkish concoction made with chick peas. Some salted cashews, a jar of mint jelly and a loaf of Russian black bread rounded out his loot.

He poured himself some sweet almond wine over the rocks, and munched and sipped and recalled.

Ruby Red.

In a purple light.

He had been working on the Dorothy Robbins case, and Steve Macker had taken him to a strip joint.

That's where he first saw Ruby Red—a stripper wearing the traditional prima ballerina costume from *Swan Lake* and doing a strip to the music. Hardy stretched and warmed to the memory as he sipped his wine.

The first thing she had bared was her hair, her beautiful red hair. Then, when the purple light changed to red, she bared her large, firm, round breasts.

Hardy erected even as he thought.

The next time he saw her was at a burlesque house in Queens.

Then that time in the tub, just before some maniac took a shot at her.

And then sprawled naked on her bed, waiting for him. . . .

And all those other times.

The time in Philadelphia, when he was working on the Walter Henry case. He could picture her in that shorty nightgown, and what she had written in eyebrow pencil on the bathroom mirror the next morning.

The doorbell rang, promising him the real thing instead of memories. He opened the door and took a long, hungry look.

"Hello, lover," she said.

As they kissed hello and he breathed in the sweet perfume of her hair, he didn't think of Faith at all—but he did think of Denise. It was Ruby's red hair that made him think of the other redhead. But it was a tiny mouse of a thought that quickly ran across the field of his brain and, just as quickly, darted down a mouse hole and away.

While he put her things in the bedroom, she chatted loudly to him while she poured herself a drink and snacked at some of the foodstuffs he had laid out.

He was back. She was sitting in the living room, in the wing chair by the window. He sprawled on the couch and was content just to look at her, for the moment.

She grinned wickedly. "Hey, stud. You getting any lately?"

"No," he answered, "I've been saving myself, just for you."

"Me, too," she said. And then she said, "I've missed you. I've missed you so much that sometimes it hurt."

Slowly he walked to the chair. He placed one finger in the cleft between those fabulous breasts and ran it up and down. She put her hand over his and pushed it closer to her. Hardy leaned over and kissed her gently. He hadn't meant it to be a whisper, but it was. "Me, too," he said.

She got up and they strolled into the bedroom, the roundness of her breast rubbing against him, as it always did when they walked together.

She never did a strip act for him. That was

only for the people who had to pay to look, but could never touch. For him she simply undressed. And as she did, he touched and caressed and kissed each new beauty she exposed.

Each marvelously exciting, agonizing second was torture and joy at the same time.

His own clothes were off before hers. Then their bodies meshed together and he was home. Home and happy, as they slithered and clamped and rocked and gyrated and went away on a private journey together, and then came back and went away for another trip.

They started up again almost immediately after they had made it the first time. Hardy was on his back, taking in visual as well as tactile pleasure.

"You have a beautiful body," he said, as she stretched, poised above him.

Even as he said it, and even as they started their second bout of lovemaking, she, in response to his flattering words, preened and pulled in her stomach just a wee bit, as if to live up to his comment. And just as a part of her sexually-oriented mind dwelt on ego and vanity, part of his dwelt on the observation of it.

He had roused himself early, and gone out for the lox and bagels and the *Times*. When he came back, they made love first.

Now, as they shared Saturday morning breakfast and read the rehash on Frank Miklos' death,

Hardy brought her up to date on everything, including Denise and Faith—it was that kind of relationship.

"Well, stud, it seems to me that you're even in the hurt and being hurt department. Forget it. As for the case, I don't know what——"

At that point, the doorbell rang furiously. Hardy turned on the tv scanner. He and Ruby exchanged kisses while the machine warmed up. The bell rang again. As it did, the tv revealed the angry, black face of Detective Gerald Friday.

Handing Ruby her robe and slipping into his, Hardy went out to let the cop in.

"Goddamn it, Hardy, have you seen the papers? This is the most fouled-up case, and it's all because of you," Friday roared, as he marched into the apartment and followed Hardy into the kitchen.

"Good morning," said Ruby. "Would you like some coffee?"

Friday stopped short at the sight of her. The lacy robe didn't leave much to the imagination. He turned to Hardy. "I'm sorry, Pat, I didn't know you had company."

Hardy chuckled. "I'll be a son of a bitch. You're embarrassed. Not only that, you're blushing. I didn't even know you could."

Friday smiled wanly.

"Coffee?" Ruby repeated.

"Yes, thank you." He stirred his sugar in, and there was silence, except for the noise his spoon made against the cup.

"Well," said Ruby, breaking the silence, "Why don't I leave you two alone to talk, and you can finish chewing him out. According to the story he's told me, he deserves it."

"Hey," said Hardy, as she sailed out, "whose side are you supposed to be on?"

Hardy turned his attention back to Friday. "In case you don't remember, that's Ruby. You met her when——"

"Will you stop with that crap? Yes, I remember her. The only thing I have against her is her friendship with you. I apologize for busting in on you like this, I didn't know ..." He let the sentence trail off into nothing. Then he started up again. "Now that the apology is out of the way, let's get to it. This is one big foul-up, and I have a strong feeling you know a lot. Talk. You're always talking about nothing, now talk about something. Talk."

Hardy went into his office, moved the George Grosz picture, and opened the safe. Friday had followed him in. Hardy tossed the passports on his desk, sat in the barber chair and waited.

When Friday had looked them over and knew what they were, Hardy said, "I found those in the loft after Miklos skipped."

"Damn! Damn! Damn! You stupid ass! I could charge you for withholding evidence."

"Hold it," said Hardy. "If you're going to charge me with something new each time I tell you something, I'll call my lawyer."

"Can that," said Friday, with exasperation. "Keep talking."

"Wait," said Hardy. "I have to get something."

Friday nodded, and looked through the passports again while Hardy went into the bedroom.

In the bedroom, Hardy started to search through his jacket pockets, but stopped in order to watch Ruby get dressed. It was almost as much fun as watching her get undressed.

"Get out of here, you Peeping Tom. Can't a girl have any privacy?"

He ducked the pillow she threw at him, and went on with his search. What the hell had he been wearing that day? He found it, took it back into the office and gave it to Friday.

"Careful," said Hardy.

"What the hell is it?"

Hardy carefully unfolded the soap wrapper. "I think if your chemist analyzed it, he would tell you that this powder is nitroglycerin—the kind that people with heart trouble take. I found it on the floor of a closet, just outside the dressing room where Lane Peterson was killed. Jackson Butler——"

"Has a heart condition," the two men said in unison.

Friday went on. "We're not complete idiots, you know. We have slips written up on each of the people who were there that day, and even on some who were not. Withholding evidence again."

"No," said Hardy. "But if stupidity is on the books, you could hold me for that. I forgot I had the damn thing in my pocket. I got involved in other things."

"It's not on the books, but with you around it should be."

"Another thing," said Hardy. "Back stairway, by the dressing room."

"We know about it," Friday snapped. "We figured all along that that's the way the killer got in and out—not like the paperbacks, where the cops are dumb and the private detective is smart, huh?"

Hardy said nothing.

"Okay," said the cop. "Just to check my supposition against yours: Butler, being in the travel business, is the first choice to be the owner of these phony passports. The girl lifted them from his clothes while he was working out, and tried to hold him up. He agreed, but when the time came, he killed her. He didn't know about the boy friend, and when Miklos tried his pitch, Butler farmed the job out and had a pro knock the kid off and dump him in Jersey."

Hardy nodded. "That's the way I see it, too."

"Anything else in your little bag you'd like to spill?"

"No, it's empty."

"You got any more coffee?" Friday asked.

Hardy nodded again, and they went back into the kitchen. Friday poured, sugared, stirred and tasted, and then shook his head. "I can't get over it. You had this stuff all along, and you knew it when I spoke with you on the phone. Well, private detective, you did it again. Maybe he wasn't too upright a citizen, but because of you, Frank Miklos is dead."

"Crap," Hardy answered. "I know I wasn't too smart about the whole thing, but the contract was probably out before we even talked."

"That still doesn't excuse you and what you did—or didn't do. It's good evidence—all circumstantial, but good. Suppose we let the D.A.'s office decide whether it's enough to bring him in, or whether we should let Butler be, and play out his line just a bit more. I don't have to tell you what I want you to do. So long. Thanks for the coffee, and tell Ruby good-bye."

"Good-bye, Gerry, and thanks."

"Good-bye, private—ah crap. See you, Pat, and take care."

That was that. They would pick up Jackson Butler within the hour and, of course,

Natasha would refuse to pay. Well, he had come out with the short end of the stick on other cases. It was only money—besides, he had Ruby.

CHAPTER THIRTEEN

⚜ That weekend was fantastic. Hardy completely forgot about the case, and Faith, and any other problems he had stored up. He and Ruby went walking, came home and made love, ate dinner, made love, watched tv, made love, read the funnies and did the *Times* crossword together, and even slept.

Holmes didn't like being excluded from certain of their activities, but enjoyed the excitement of having someone else in the house to make a fuss over him. On Sunday, Ruby was doing just that, while Hardy watched *Kiss Me Kate* on television. Hardy was singing along with Keenan Wynn and James Whitmore as they did "Brush Up Your Shakespeare," when Holmes decided to join in, too.

The poodle sat on his haunches and barked

his way into a howl, to coincide with the ending of the song. Ruby got hysterical.

"I didn't know he could do that."

"Neither did I," said Hardy. "He's never done it before." He turned off the tv. "I'm going to sing it again."

And he did, and so did Holmes.

Then the three of them curled up on the couch to watch the rest of the movie, until two of them kicked one of them off to make love again.

Monday morning, after breakfast, Ruby went off to see some friends, and Hardy started to collect the info he had gathered on the Lane Peterson case to store it in the file room.

He answered the phone before Holmes could bark at it.

"Trouble Limited, Patrick Hardy speaking."

"Pat, this is Gerry Friday. A word to the wise. The D.A.'s office has decided not to pick up Jackson Butler yet. We're supposed to wait and see if they can get a really air-tight case. Cautious people over there. If it was up to me, I'd have picked him up on Saturday, and wrapped him in a package then and there. You were right about that powder you gave me—but forget all that. Now, here's my word to the wise: remember what I said to you on Saturday?"

"Yeah."

"Well, now it goes double." He hung up

without bothering to say good-bye, as was his general custom.

Hardy's mind started churning. His mental tape recorder replayed exactly what Friday had said: "... I don't have to tell you what I want you to do. So long..."

Hardy listened to Friday's parting remarks over and over in his mind. There had been no specific mention of staying off the case, he rationalized to himself. If he could beat the city to the conclusive evidence needed to nail Butler, he could still earn his fee. But where to look?

He ignored Holmes' barking as he rushed about getting dressed. The dog, who always reflected Hardy's mood, sensed that something was up and wanted to be in on it. The annoyed bark was even more pronounced when Hardy left the apartment without him, and without having taken him on his morning run in the park.

Hardy's first action was like the proverbial chicken with its head cut off. He got into a cab and, when the driver asked where to, only then did he figure out the answer.

"Public library."

"Which one, Mac? There's a lot of them, you know."

"Forty-Second Street." He lit a cigarette and sat hunched forward for the entire trip downtown.

In the library, he looked through the scanner at reduced copies of the *Times*. He read through recent and not so recent magazines. He found what he wanted, but it only confirmed what he knew in a general way; there was nothing specific he could lay his hands on that would help him get the goods on Jackson Butler.

A magazine article mentioned an organization man involved in drugs, calling him a "multi-passport personality who lived in Switzerland and who was able to enter and leave the United States with the ease of a man going through a revolving door."

Another story told of a man in the stolen-car business who had his home base in Canada and was the owner of several passports bearing different names.

A newspaper item mentioned that the market value of a good forged passport for escapees or refugees from the Orient, the Arab countries or Russia was five thousand dollars, and up.

Good for what it was, but not good enough for Hardy's purposes.

He left the library and resisted the impulse to duck into a movie and hide from the problem. His stomach did not resist, though. After gobbling down a frankfurter and a coke, he stopped at an adjacent stand and ate a slice of pizza and washed it down with a root beer. He belched silently and lit a cigarette.

He was near Sandy Josephs' office. Maybe

there was something there he had overlooked. He didn't know if he was right, but he was desperate. Any port in a storm, he clichéd to himself.

Josephs wasn't in. Hardy tried to get something out of the receptionist, but she was so busy with her personal calls, he doubted if even Josephs got too much out of her.

Hardy kept waiting around, hoping that Josephs would show, or that the girl would put down the phone long enough to answer questions. Finally, the icky part of the conversations he was privy to got to be too much, and he let himself out. Before the door closed, he peeked back in, but she was still talking and had never even noticed he was gone.

Hardy wondered if she had really noticed he'd been there. Well, that was Josephs' problem, not his. His were of a bigger nature. How the hell was he going to nail Jackson Butler?

He stopped at a pay phone and called his friend Joan at the Glory Travel Service.

Joan Verdetasse told him she was free, and to come on over. Hardy hopped a cab to the East Side and was there in ten minutes. Joan was a statuesque brunette who had definite possibilities as an object of his lechery but, unfortunately, she was married to a friend of Hardy's. However, it was Hardy's good sense rather than his conscience that kept Joan off his list of prospectives.

She bounced up from her desk and pecked him on the mouth. "Hi, sweetie, what can I do for you? Paris? Rome? Samarkand?"

"I want to ask you about one of your colleagues."

"Here in the office?"

"No, a fellow-traveller travel agent."

"Pat, that's corny."

"I know, but I'm coming to the end of a long piece of string, and there's nothing on it."

"What?"

"Never mind, Joan. Come on, I'll take you to lunch, and you can tell me all you know about Jackson Butler."

"There's nothing much to tell."

Joan was right. She didn't have much to tell. But Hardy did enjoy her company, and they enjoyed the crepes, and he considered the possibilities of her husband being transferred by his firm to Samarkand.

After Hardy dropped Joan back at her office, he decided to visit Jackson Butler's travel agency. He walked the several blocks and, despite his situation, enjoyed the day and the weather and all the pretty girls who were in view.

Butler wasn't in. Hardy didn't know if he was glad or sorry about that. All he got for his troubles was a handful of travel folders. As he looked for a litter basket in which to deposit them, an idea passed through his thinking mechanism that Sandy Josephs and Jackson Butler both being out might be more than a coincidence. But Josephs' absence had been almost an hour before.

Hardy hit another pay phone, got Sandy Josephs' number from information, and dialed it. The *non-compos-mentis* at the other end told him that Mr. Josephs was out, and that she didn't know when he would be back. Interesting, thought Hardy, but then he didn't know what else to make of it or do about it.

He roamed about, looking in windows and at women, and at various books in various types of bookstores, trying at the same time to avoid the problem and to goose his mind into getting on the right track that would help him solve the problem. He bought two science-fiction books, one mystery, one porno, one religious.

Ruby wasn't at home when he got there, so he took Holmes across the street to the park and sat on a bench that was almost directly opposite his apartment doorway while the animal did dog things in the grass.

Lost in his plans, or lack of them, he didn't even notice Ruby approaching and sitting down—and that, he thought, is really being out of it.

"Hi, stud. How goes it?"

"It doesn't go. You have to push it."

She kissed him lightly. "Honestly, Pat, I wish you would get some new material."

"You keep handing me those straight lines. I have to come back with the killers."

"Yes," she said. "But this time you don't have the killer."

He squinted at her to see if the remark was innocent or if she was putting him on. She was putting him on.

"Don't have the killer! Talk about lousy material! Stick to *Floogle Street* and bits you know. Wait till I get you inside."

She stuck her tongue in his ear and whispered, "Talk, talk, talk, nothing but talk."

They went back to the apartment.

Afterwards, as they lay sprawled in bed, looking and just grooving on each others' bodies, he said, "How would you like to go out to dinner tonight?"

"I'd love it," she answered. "But don't you think you ought to cool it?" she added, as she took a firm grasp on a hunk of his developing spare tire.

He nodded and didn't get angry. "You're right. Starting tomorrow, I'll go on a diet. But tonight we dine at——Nero's. Wait till you taste their lobster."

Hardy loved going places with Ruby. Men actually stumbled over their feet when they turned to stare at her. Some women were disconcerted, too.

He looked around to see if Gary Thorpe or Ralph Price or any of the other regulars were in the place, and was surprised to see Faith Cade and Sandy Josephs sitting at a table in the corner.

Ruby touched the back of his neck and said, under her breath, "From the way you just tensed up, and the way a certain blonde is staring at us, I'd give ten to one that that certain blonde is Faith Cade."

"No bet," said Hardy. "The guy with her is Sandy Josephs. I've been trying to see him all day."

"Well, now's your chance."

Hardy hesitated. "You mean, just walk over?"

"Of course," said Ruby. "*Noblesse oblige.* It's your duty to go over and congratulate the happy couple on their engagement—even buy them a bottle of wine. Then they'll invite us to join them at their table. They won't mean it, but we'll accept, and there we are."

Hardy shook his head at the maître d' and, like a soldier following a battle plan, he paraded over to that table in the corner.

"Hello, Faith, Mr. Josephs." He thrust out his hand to Sandy Josephs. "Congratulations."

"Thank you," said Josephs.

He passed names around and called the waiter over. As the waiter approached, Hardy said to Faith and her fiancé, "If you don't mind, it would be my pleasure to offer some wine, by way of celebration."

The waiter was there. Hardy turned to him. "A bottle of Dom Perignon——"

"I know," said the waiter, who recognized him, " '59." And he scurried off to fetch the champagne.

"That's very nice of you," Faith Cade said.

"Yes," agreed Sandy Josephs. "Would you care to join us?"

"We'd love to," said Ruby, doing her share of the work.

Following that, Hardy, Faith Cade and Sandy Josephs had a very uncomfortable evening, while Hardy learned nothing that would help his case. Ruby, who kept ordering more champagne, had the time of her life.

She giggled all the way home in the cab while Hardy fretted over what an ass he had made of himself.

He could hear Holmes barking from outside on the street. Hardy quickly paid off the driver and tried to rush in, but with all the locks he had to contend with, it was sort of difficult.

Once inside, Holmes led them to the source of his irritation. A pipe had burst in the master bathroom, and the water level was slowly rising. Hardy ran in and rescued a favorite bamboo cabinet, soaking his feet going in and nearly trampling Ruby and Holmes coming out.

Using the house phone, he called the doorman to connect him with the superintendent. It was after midnight, and the man, who had never in his three years on the job, met Hardy, refused to put the call through.

Hardy slammed the house phone down and stalked out of the apartment and around to the main entrance. He marched in, ignoring the doorman, and rang the bell of the superintendent's ground-floor apartment.

A quiet, balding man opened the door and said, pleasantly, "Hello, Mr. Hardy. What can I do for you?" He seemed not at all put out by the lateness of his caller.

Hardy was half annoyed and half drunk. "Get me an ark, and provisions for forty days."

"Huh?"

"I've got a flood in the bathroom, Vic, you've got to do something."

"Okay, Mr. Hardy, I'll come around and take a look."

When they had mopped up most of the water, and Vic had turned off the proper valves, and had helped Hardy place buckets in strategic areas, and had roused the plumber, who grudgingly promised to be there if there were no emergencies that took priority, it was several hours later.

"No emergencies?" said a beaten Hardy. "What does he think this is? Chopped liver?"

Ruby giggled, and Vic told them good night.

Hardy stood there, the water from his drenched pants dripping on the rug. His ear caught the different patterns of sound as he heard different droplets of water falling into different buckets. "Jesus Christ. Now we're going to have to listen to that all night."

By this time, Ruby was laughing so violently that she had to sit on the bed and hold her stomach. "I hate to say this, Pat," she cut off a laugh and gasped for breath, then looked at him again and started laughing again. "I really hate to say this, considering what a day it's been, but after all the bad one-liners you've pulled on me, you deserve it."

Hardy managed a brave face and a tiny smile. "Okay."

"Patrick Hardy, you're all wet."

"That's the most ridiculous statement I've ever heard," he Groucho'd back. And they both laughed hysterically while he rid himself of his wet clothes and nearly ripped off hers, and they made love all night long to the drip, drip, drip of the leak.

CHAPTER FOURTEEN

※ The plumbers came bright and early, much too early for Hardy's libido. Ruby took their appearance as an excuse to escape and go shopping. Hardy ate some overcooked oatmeal and sat at his desk, trying to concentrate while the plumbers gleefully hammered away and made guesses as to where the source of the leak was.

Eventually, they found it and repaired it, and even cleaned up most of the mess.

Hardy spent some time with Vic, arranging for the plasterer to come by and patch the gaping holes.

"And what about the painter?"

"First, let's get the holes fixed, Mr. Hardy, okay? One thing at a time."

"Right, Vic. Thanks for everything."

One thing at a time. Vic was right. One thing at a time. And the next one thing for him to do was to go downtown to Natasha's and take his next therapy session.

For some reason that he couldn't quite fathom, he was excitedly calm as his cab took him towards the studio. Excitedly calm—what was that word that designated contradictory ideas coupled together? Buckley always used it in his column. He'd have to remember to look it up when he got home.

"Oxymoron," he said to the driver, remembering the word just as he paid him off.

"What was that?"

"Nothing. Nothing at all," said Hardy only then realizing that he had blurted it out, and what it must have sounded like to the driver. "Have a nice day."

"Wise guy," said the cabbie, and roared away.

Upstairs, as he changed clothes, Hardy had what he felt to be a strained conversation with Jackson Butler but, reconsidering it as he went into the studio to work out, Butler was the same nice, sweet man he had seemed to be all the times before.

Faith was working with another client. They exchanged half-smiles with each other, and then Hardy settled down to let Carmen take him through his paces.

Natasha came over and shooed Carmen away. "No, Mr. Hardy, you are doing it all wrong. You see what happens when you skip a time. You should never skip a session. It only means that you have to start the process all over again. It is never good to interrupt therapy." Then she lowered her voice, if Natasha could ever have been said to lower her voice, "What is your progress on the case?"

Hardy groaned as his thigh muscles were pulled to their extreme, and more, "I almost have it. As a matter of fact, I should be wrapping it up in about a week."

Natasha nodded at the information and corrected the position of Hardy's legs on the current exercise.

As they changed clothes again, Mr. Butler said, "You should never skip a session. It hurts twice as much that way. Excuse me, Mr. Hardy, but could I trouble you for a cigarette?"

Hardy looked askance.

"Oh, I know I'm not supposed to. But every once in a while, when I feel good, I think it's all right to break a rule. And today I feel wonderful. What are your thoughts about breaking rules, Mr. Hardy?"

Hardy handed the man a cigarette and, taking one for himself, lit them both. They were alone in the dressing room.

"I'm afraid I don't quite follow, Mr. Butler."

"Well, actually, what I'm doing is posing an abstract question in ethics: how do you feel about breaking rules?"

Hardy was perplexed. Was the man just holding aimless conversation, or was he aware of Hardy's suspicions and seeing whether he could buy him off.

"That depends on a great many things, Mr. Butler."

The older man shook his head from side to side, but said, "Yes, I suppose it does. For instance?"

"What do you mean, for instance?"

Butler smoked like a person who had never smoked at all. "Well, if you asked me for a for-instance, I would say it's all right to break a rule when the rule is wrong, or when the rule you break is only detrimental to those with twisted values and concepts."

"That's a very interesting theory," said Hardy. "But I'm afraid I just don't see it that way."

"What a pity. I was afraid you might think that. Thank you very much for the cigarette, and thank you for this little talk. It's been most enlightening."

"Don't mention it, I'm sure," said Hardy, and he rushed through his dressing and left the room.

Faith was waiting for him when he came out.

"That was a dirty trick you played on me last night, Patrick Hardy."

"What do you mean?" he asked. He really didn't know what she meant.

"You know—you and your friend putting us on like that last night. Though I must say, I deserved it. It was a dirty trick to pull on you, the way I told you about my engagement. Wow! You certainly don't sit around and mope, do you? Here I was, sure I had broken your heart, and you show up with someone like Ruby Red. She is one of the most magnificent women I have ever seen."

"Thanks. I'll tell her you said so."

"You do, and I'll scratch your eyes out and deny I ever said it. Damn it, Pat, I hope some day I'm not sorry."

"What?" he asked, the hairs on the back of his neck rising.

"No," said Faith. "Nothing. Stupid remark. Never said it. You never heard it."

She kissed him on the cheek and took his hand.

"Friends?" she said.

"Sure thing—but I don't think I'll be coming here much longer."

"You, too? All my favorites are leaving."

"Wait a minute, Faith. What do you mean by that?"

"First Mr. Butler, now you."

"What's that about Mr. Butler?"

"Well, he and Natasha were in the office. I guess they didn't see me. I guess it has something to do with his heart."

"Go on, go on," said Hardy, impatiently.

"Nothing much more to say. He was telling her that he was going to go and live in South America, that it would be a more healthy place for him to be."

"I'll say it would," Hardy answered, and just then Jackson Butler came out of the dressing room and walked towards the elevator. Hardy didn't say a word to Faith but trailed behind the little man, wondering what to do.

The only thing he could think of was to say something, and he did.

"Why don't you use the back stairs, Mr. Butler?"

The quiet little man turned around and said, very calmly, "I beg your pardon, Mr. Hardy?"

"I said, why don't you use the back stairs, the way you did the day you killed Lane Peterson?"

Faith gasped, and he thought he heard noises from Carmen and Natasha.

"Is this your idea of a joke, Mr. Hardy? If it is, I assure you, I don't find it a funny one."

Natasha broke in. "Mr. Hardy, how dare you insult Mr. Butler? I fire you from the case. Mr. Butler, I think you should leave. I won't have one of my people subjected to this sort of insolence and embarrassment."

"Fine with me, Natasha," Hardy answered. "I'm fired. But my services always end at midnight of the last day of employment, so you still have more time coming to you.

"Don't leave, Mr. Butler. Let's finish our conversation about ethics. Is it within your scope of ethical behavior to commit murder, Mr. Butler? You know you gave it away yourself, even before I had any physical evidence against you. The way you made a remark about Lane Peterson and her twisted values, and then, when we went out to dinner, you kept harping on that same phrase, pretending that you meant it about all the kids of this generation. You knew you had made a slip of the tongue and tried to cover it up. I must say, you did a good job, too. I missed it completely. Boy, was I dense."

Butler leaned against the wall. "And now I presume you are being clear-headed. I must warn you, Mr. Hardy, if you persist in this attack I shall sue you. I have more than enough witnesses."

"Tell me, Mr. Butler, were you this cool when you were waiting to kill her? I doubt that very much. Otherwise, why would you have needed one of your pills?"

Hardy waited for some response, but since none was forthcoming, he continued. "There was some powder in the closet. I scraped it up and had it analyzed. According to the report, it was nitroglycerin. What sort of heart medicine do you use, Butler? Was it the anticipation of murder, or was it the long climb up those stairs that made you need the pill?

"Frank Miklos is gone, but he left some passports behind that lead straight to you. Lane stole the passports from your coat, or found them there, or something. Whatever happened, she had them, and she knew they were worth money to you if you could get them back without anybody ever knowing about them. When she told you what she wanted, you agreed. But then, after checking her schedule on the board in the office, and realizing when she'd be in the dressing room, changing her clothes to leave, you sneaked up the back stairs and waited in the closet until she was in there alone. You also knew from the schedule that no one was due in or out for the next half hour, and that no men were scheduled at all. You changed the dial to read 'Male,' and went in and murdered her.

"After you killed her, you changed the sign back and left, and came back later at your normal time. I have to admit, you handled yourself well while we were dressing."

Butler kept his position against the wall and said nothing, but took in several rapid breaths.

Hardy was desperate. The man was out-acting him. He had to keep on talking.

"I should have known by that look on your face when you came off the elevator and saw me coming out of the stairwell. I thought it was normal surprise, but you knew it meant that I had figured out how the killer had come in, and that I was getting closer to you. Who knows? Up until then, you might have gone on paying off Frank Miklos, but I doubt it. You didn't know about him when you killed Lane. You thought she was in it by herself. Anyway, you got smart after that, and called a number and sent out a contract on Miklos. Your second murder was a lot more professional than your first. If you had killed the girl the same way, I might never have tumbled. Or was it your second murder? Have there been others? Was this your third? Or your tenth? Maybe you enjoyed looking at her nude body as you strangled the life out of her."

The room was deathly quiet. Hardy paused, and a thought that had been poised on the precipice of his mind leaped in.

"Though how you managed to choke and then lift a healthy girl like Lane Peterson is beyond me."

Butler was gasping for air. He gave a garbled cry. "Natasha!"

"Shut up, you fool!"

Hardy turned to stare at Natasha, whose face was livid with rage.

Of course, thought Hardy, the studio gave her entree to many people. She and Butler were partners. She'd probably killed Lane, with Butler acting as lookout—or had they done it together?

While Hardy's jumbled mind was busy cogitating, Natasha's hand went to a hidden spot in the cubbyhole office and came out holding a gun.

Butler was on the floor, gurgling and trying to reach his gold pill box. Carmen went to help him.

"Leave him," Natasha screamed. "The little fool! Just like you, Mr. Hardy—you're a fool, too. You have all the correct facts, and all of the incorrect conclusions." She pointed to Butler's convulsing body. "If he had told me that Lane had the passports, I would have warned him about Miklos. I knew that she didn't do a thing without telling that scum. But Butler, my partner, Butler, the fool, had to try to take care of it himself—a task he wasn't at all up to. A weakling and a fool. I hate weaklings and fools. When I came into the dressing room, Lane had almost killed him. I strangled her myself, and put her in the shower. I am not a weakling. I'm still a very strong woman, and I'm over sixty years old. How many women of my age do you know are in as good a shape as I?

"As for you, Mr. Hardy—you, the other fool—Butler didn't drop his pills in the closet while waiting for Lane to go into the dressing room to change. He dropped them there afterwards, where I hid him until he recovered sufficiently so I could sneak him down the back stairs, the way he had come.

"Did you know I was a very respected performer in Europe? But I think my best performance ever was when you showed me the body. Don't you agree, Mr. Hardy?"

Hardy was mesmerized. He was damned if he knew what to do now—and he was a bit afraid that Natasha was going to shoot him.

Suddenly, Faith chopped at Natasha's gun hand, disarming her, and then clipped the woman on the jaw, putting her out.

"I've been wanting to do that for a long time." She turned to Hardy. "I told you I took karate. Pretty good, huh?"

He glanced to make sure that Natasha was no problem and ran over to Jackson Butler. He was dead.

"Heart attack," said Hardy. Even as he said them, the words sounded fake, out of a bad *Late-Late-Show* movie. He jiggled the gold pill box in his hand and then placed it back on the floor.

Despite everything Butler may have done, Hardy was feeling guilt pangs about the little man's death. He shoved the thoughts far away and stood up.

"Thanks, friend," he said to Faith, and went to the pay phone to dial a familiar number.

CHAPTER FIFTEEN

❈ The smell of fresh plaster that had permeated the apartment had been replaced by the odors of homemade *vichyssoise*, filet of flounder almondine, strawberry mousse, strong coffee and good brandy.

Hardy and Ruby were snuggling while an FM station played Brubeck, and Holmes tried to get his share of brandy and attention.

"Ruby?"

"What, lover?"

"Ask me how I figured the case out."

"Better question: how are you going to get paid?"

"I might be able to get something from Natasha's lawyers. Now ask me how I figured the case out."

"But I know how. You found the passports, and the powder in the closet and——"

"No. Just ask me how I knew."

"All right, Mr. Bones. How did you know who did it?"

"Simple," he said, trying to imitate Cary Grant. "In all the best murder mysteries, the Butler always did it."

"Oh for——" and she hit him with a pillow. "——it's a good thing I dig your body, Patrick Hardy. You have the mind of a ten-year-old. I adore the way you climb my bones, but I wish you would forget about being a comic."

Hardy switched to his Groucho Marx act. "Say that again about my body, and I'll hold you to it."

Ruby finished her brandy and tousled his hair, "Oh, shut up and let's go to bed."

AUTHORS GUILD BACKINPRINT.COM EDITIONS are fiction and nonfiction works that were originally brought to the reading public by established United States publishers but have fallen out of print. The economics of traditional publishing methods force tens of thousands of works out of print each year, eventually claiming many, if not most, award-winning and one-time best-selling titles. With improvements in print-on-demand technology, authors and their estates, in cooperation with the Authors Guild, are making some of these works available again to readers in quality paperback editions. Authors Guild Backinprint.com Editions may be found at nearly all online bookstores and are also available from traditional booksellers. For further information or to purchase any Backinprint.com title please visit www.backinprint.com.

Except as noted on their copyright pages, Authors Guild Backinprint.com Editions are presented in their original form. Some authors have chosen to revise or update their works with new information. The Authors Guild is not the editor or publisher of these works and is not responsible for any of the content of these editions.

THE AUTHORS GUILD is the nation's largest society of published book authors. Since 1912 it has been the leading writers' advocate for fair compensation, effective copyright protection, and free expression. Further information is available at www.authorsguild.org.

Please direct inquiries about the Authors Guild and Backinprint.com Editions to the Authors Guild offices in New York City, or e-mail staff@backinprint.com.

Printed in the United States
64924LVS00001B/28